THE DEVIL WA~~LKS IN BLOOD~~
BOOK TWO

SPECIAL EDITION

INCLUDES THE NOVELETTE
DEAD MAN WALKING
NICK HOLLERAN SERIES

HELL IN HAVEN CITY URBAN FANTASY

EERIE RIVER PUBLISHING
www.EerieRiverPublishing.com

Eerie River Publishing
www.EerieRiverPublishing.com
Hamilton, Ontario Canada

This book is a work of fiction. Names, characters, places, events, organi-
zations and incidents are either part of the author's imagination or
are used fictitiously. Any resemblance to actual persons, living or dead,
or actual events is purely coincidental. Except all the details about Hell,
that is real.

Paperback ISBN: 978-1-990245-41-1
Digital ISBN: 978-1-990245-06-0
Second Edition 2021
Dead Man Walking & The Devil Walks In Blood

Edited by S.O. Green and Michelle River
Cover design by Grady Earls
https://www.artstation.com/gradyearls
Book Formatting by Michelle River

ALSO BY DAVID GREEN

Dead Man Walking

A Place Beyond the Storm

In Solitude's Shadow

Path of War

Never miss a new release!
Follow David on his Facebook page and
sign up for his newsletter.

https://www.facebook.com/davidgreenwriter

To Marie and Ollie, the wisdom and mischief in my life.

CONTENTS

FOREWORD   9

DEAD MAN WALKING   13

THE DEVIL WALKS IN BLOOD   91

AUTHOR DAVID GREEN   269

To Gr[...]

Happy Reading!

D[...]

FOREWORD

Welcome to Haven City.

You can find all kinds of things in this sprawling metropolis, if you look hard enough. Strange things, dangerous things, the kind of things no one wants to admit they've seen out loud. But you can't turn a blind eye once you've seen it. Once you've lived it. Maybe, just maybe, there's someone you can hire to help make sense of it all.

Hell is real. We're all living it. Nick Holleran learned that truth the hard way the day he took three bullets to the chest and bled out in an alleyway. Only death didn't stick, and it's been five long years working among the ghosts and monsters, demons and fallen angels, hoping that next time he'll make it to heaven.

But things are never that simple, are they?

This series follows the trials and tribulations, the blood, sweat and tears, of Haven's one and only Paranormal Investigator as he struggles with his place in a world inhabited by both the living and the dead.

In this Special Edition of The Devil Walks in Blood, you'll find the original Nick Holleran novelette, Dead Man Walking, included as bonus content.

The Devil Walks in Blood picks up right where we left off in Dead Man Walking, making this the perfect all-in-one book.

Sit back, pour yourself a whiskey, and get ready to see the world through a dead man's eyes. In Hell, things aren't always what they seem.

~ Michelle, Eerie River Publishing

"Through me you go into a city of weeping; through me you go into eternal pain; through me you go amongst the lost people."

~ Dante Alighieri, The Inferno

DEAD MAN WALKING
BOOK ONE

How it all began...

PROLOGUE

You might say life changed the day I died.

Can't say I saw it coming, but the end comes for us all, right? Not how I'd imagined it, lying in a dirty alleyway with three gaping holes in my chest. I went from bleeding rivers in the gutter to floating above my body, draped in warm, bright light. Confusion and regret shot through my consciousness as I watched my white shirt blooming crimson and tears leaking from my own unseeing eyes.

Watching yourself die? Don't recommend it.

Regret only grew when a woman—a complete stranger—raced to my side, her long, cashmere coat wicking filth from the floor of the alley. I watched, helpless, as she shrugged off that fancy coat and pressed it to the wounds, holding the blood inside that sack of meat and bones. Her dark eyes stayed focused, despite the panic.

Her voice called to me, told me to hold on.

The light around me grew brighter, warmer. No words, but I understood. Heaven? Me? Never thought I'd be the type. Wouldn't say I believed, and I enjoyed my share of vices. Go figure.

Below, my body pulled at me as the woman staunched the bleeding and turned to dial 911. She wouldn't let me die without a fight and I hovered there, between life and death. I didn't want to go back to that broken shell, to the life I'd left behind, but I couldn't move on. She wouldn't let me. Hell, I wouldn't let me. I refused to lie down among the trash and give in.

The light sang to me...right up until it didn't. The paramedics coaxed my body back to life. They coaxed *me* back into my body. She'd kept me alive long enough to save me. A miracle, they told her.

I'm not so sure.

What happens to a man once he knows Heaven exists, and that he missed out? That, if it hadn't been for the kindness of strangers and skill of healthcare professionals, he could've gone to that bright and beautiful afterlife and left all this behind?

The day I left the hospital—after operations, rehabilitation, and a bill I'll be paying the rest of my second life—I discovered Hell exists too.

We're living there.

SPECTRES OF THE PAST

SEPTEMBER 20th
HAVEN CITY, OREGON

It's been five years to the day since I died.

Looking through my office window, two stories above Main Street, I raise a tumbler of Jack Daniels to the grey heavens looming above Haven.

"Hey, big guy. It's Nick Holleran. Here's to ya, you sonofabitch."

The drink goes down smooth, and the familiar heat burning up my throat is only soured a little by the thought of the warmth I could have had. I'm not an alcoholic; I only drink on special occasions. That's what they all say, right? But the fifth anniversary of your own death? That's pretty special.

Liquor would be an easy crutch to lean on, and a drunk private investigator is just too perfect an image. Maybe I'll sink towards a walking cliché at some point down the road, but not today. Have to keep my wits about me.

I don't need the black clouds glaring down at me or that greasy feeling in the air to tell me there's a storm coming. I can smell it, and I don't mean the weather. Haven's stirring, and it's making me antsy.

With a sigh, I turn back to my cramped, dingy office. Like me, it's seen better days. Suspicious stains, peeling here and there, full of holes, and the office ain't much better. But, hey, it's home.

In the corner, an adolescent girl—I call her Darcy and she's never corrected me—stands with her back to me, staring at...something, I guess. When I got back from the hospital, there she stood, between the sofa and a bookshelf with more bills than novels on it. Her dark, pigtailed hair falls past her slumped shoulders. She could've stood there for years for all I know—I try not to think about it—and God knows her clothes look the part. She's wearing a one-piece dress that ain't from this decade.

She's never uttered a word to me. The first day I saw her, I asked where her parents were and pulled her round to face me. Her eyeless stare sent me scrambling straight back into my desk. Congealed blood crusted her cheeks, her mouth hanging open and slack. In silence, she turned away and resumed her study of the wall and she hasn't stopped since.

Not a lot of folks can see 'Darcy.' I try to ignore her now. She's part of the furniture, though if I'm honest, I find myself watching her sometimes—nights like this especially—wondering what her story is.

"To five years of friendship, kiddo," I call, raising my glass.

She ignores me. Of course she does.

It didn't start with her. That first morning, staggering

out of St. Mary's Hospital, legs protesting after weeks of disuse, I ended up here, at the office. Closer than my apartment and, truth be told, I spent a Hell—pardon the expression—of a lot more time there. The streets felt jammed with people, like the population of Haven had exploded the moment they wheeled me into the ER.

It took me a few minutes to figure it out. Some detective, huh? Let's blame the painkillers.

Everywhere I looked, I saw them. Filling the sidewalks. Standing in the street. Leaning out the windows. Ghosts. Hundreds of 'em.

Grey shadows, with the living passing by them, even *through* them, oblivious. The dead just lingering, drifting without purpose for the most part. I stumbled down Main Street, mouth hanging opening. I'd have thought I'd died too if the pain in my chest and the aching in my legs didn't remind me otherwise. Some of the ghosts looked my way, others carried on with whatever business the dead have, but me? I dragged myself straight to my office.

"I'm alive," I told myself. Over and over.

I knew the docs had repaired the damage done to my body, but maybe the bullets had broken my mind. You can hallucinate from blood loss, right? Or maybe a reaction to pain meds?

Then I ran into *him*, waiting outside my apartment, and realized that Haven had more than just ghosts walking its streets.

He dressed all in black, with a cloak to match, craggy, stoic face peering from under his hood, more bone than skin. Black pits for eyes that I couldn't bring myself to meet.

The guy looked like an undead Clint Eastwood.

Charon, the ferryman, the keeper of souls. Yeah, the one from legend. The dude who carries the dead across the River Styx. Anubis. The Grim Reaper. Dulahan. All the same bastard, and that bastard's name is Charon.

I'm paraphrasing, but that's the same introduction he gave me. My reaction?

"I ain't dead."

Let me tell you a secret. The sonofabitch set a chill in my bones like nothing I've ever felt, before or since. And that includes my blood gushing out through three matching holes. Light seemed to bend around him, pulling my eyes to him and only him. Time ceased to matter as I waited for him to speak again. Maybe it took years, and the world just held its breath for him.

Sure as shit, I hated standing in front of him. Hated it deep.

"You should be," Charon said, teeth bared in a skeleton snarl. "Your fate has changed. Most vexing when destiny does not follow the course."

"Sure," I muttered, glancing around the sidewalk. "Nothing worse."

Regular folk passed by, oblivious. Just like I'd been. A few gave me the side-eye, and I understood. They couldn't see him, which left me talking to myself.

Charon leaned into me and he whispered something. God as my witness, I know he did, and the words made my blood run cold, made my lungs deflate and my heart clench for a split-second. Then they slipped from my mind. Gone.

At times, I lie awake, trying to remember what he said.

I've seen him from time-to-time since, and those words threaten to bloom into my mind. But they don't. They're always there, out of reach, just beyond my goddamn fingertips. Like I said, he's a bastard.

"Be seeing you," the ferryman breathed. More like a death rattle.

I raced up the stairs to my office, legs protesting every step, fumbled the key into the lock and slammed the door behind me, desperate for something normal. Something familiar. I gulped air, drank it in, then had a better idea. The bottle of Jack Daniels on my desk beckoned me, sang my name. I stumbled over, afraid to glance anywhere else, and filled a glass. I'd been dry for weeks. Figured I deserved a drink.

Crashing into my seat, that's when I saw her. 'Darcy'. Skin and clothes all grey and washed out, standing in the corner, staring at the wall.

You know the rest.

When my heart stopped trying to break my ribcage, I retreated to my chair, bourbon in my shaking hand.

"Ghosts out there," I muttered, downing my drink and pouring another, "in here too. Welcome to Hell, Nick."

When you're right, you're right. Each day, I ventured out to discover this new Haven I found myself in. My P.I. skills came in handy. There are folk like me out there, but I've had to search to discover them. Our 'talent' isn't something we like to shout about. The ones who talk end up institutionalized, or worse. Funny thing though. The ones who shout are free and easy and in all the weirdest corners of the internet.

Quacks, I used to call them. Fuck me, right?

I tracked down folks like Harry and Maeve—good people who knew the truth and stopped me going nuts—and hubs like the Styx Bar where I could learn the ropes. They helped me see Hell for what it is, and find my place in it.

Thank my lucky stars I did. Hell's a dangerous place for a curious type like me.

It's funny. The Pacific Northwest contains the highest number of atheists in the USA. I used to be an 'aggressive nonbeliever'—I've got my mom to thank for sticking that label on me.

Now, you could say I'm a zealot. The afterlife exists. Heaven is up there, waiting for some of us when we die. Thing is, Hell isn't below our feet. Maybe there are nine layers, like Dante wrote, but I know this for sure: Hell is Earth.

I see them wherever I go. Ghosts, demons, and anything else I read about in the Bible or storybooks. Some know they're here and can affect the living. Others can't or just plain don't.

The myths and legends you've read about? Real. Every one. Including Bigfoot. Although his feet don't look so big in person.

Sighing, I rub at the knots of scar tissue under my shirt and turn away from the only guest at my anniversary celebration, back to the window and the streets of Haven below. The clouds have split and rain's driving to the ground.

The ghosts don't mind.

Scentless Apprentice by Nirvana crunches out of the speakers on my desk. An angry, ol' song but hey, five years ago I cheated death, cheated myself out of my reward. I can be angsty if I want. My fingers drum to the pounding rhythm, and I skip back and play it again when it ends.

Listen, I'm from Oregon. Grunge music is in my blood, and I enjoy rewinding to my teenage years. I have a little stereotype in me after all. Doesn't everyone?

It's getting dark out. Rain swirls in the air, driven this way and that by the Fall wind. Down on the sidewalk, my eyes are drawn to a woman in a black mask, hood drawn up. She pauses and glances up at my window before ducking in through the entrance. I fill my mouth with Jack Daniels again.

Sue me, it's Friday.

I kept up the P.I. work. Why not? What else would I do, and I got bills to pay like every other living soul, though my cases veer more towards the paranormal these days. You might wonder why I'm still here at all, now I know the truth. Why not end it, disappear on through the big, old pearl gates above?

It's like this—I want to go upstairs when I die. Can't kill myself. I've seen too much to realize the priests and fanatics were correct about suicide. So, I help people, keep my slate nice and clean, and try to figure out an answer to the greatest questions: Why did humanity wind up living in Hell? Is this how it's always been? Or did we do something to deserve our fate?

So far, I've got nada.

Footsteps outside my office door tell me the woman from the street is about to enter. She hesitates. They always do. I flick off Nirvana, ready to give my newest client my full attention.

I glance at Darcy. I don't think she's a fan of grunge. She's never complained, but I swear her shoulders slump a little when I listen to it. Each time someone enters my office, I wonder if they'll be able to see her too.

The door swings open and in she walks. Tall, thin, draped in an expensive coat, hood still drawn up despite coming in from the rain. It covers her hair and most of her face. Eyes shimmering like polished bronze peer at me over the top of the mask.

She's wearing long gloves too, like it's the height of a pandemic. She pauses next to the ghost in the corner and, for a second, I hold my breath.

"Nick Holleran?" she asks, voice muffled by the mask.

"You know there hasn't been an outbreak for a while, right?" I say, pointing to the chair opposite. "Don't worry though, the seat's at least two meters away and I wipe it between clients. Old habits die hard, huh?"

Her eyes narrow at my remark, but she sits down anyway. Staring at me, she strips off the gloves. The skin beneath is gnarled and twisted, like acid stripped the flesh from her hands. Next, the mask comes off, and even though I half-expect what I'll see, my heart goes out to her.

A scar runs from ear-to-ear, straight through the corners of her mouth. Her lips look chewed up, shredded, like she's been force-fed glass. I stare into those beautiful eyes of hers and she looks back without flinching, tall and poised in her chair. Despite the scars, there's strength there, cold as iron and just as hard.

Or maybe it's *because* of the scars.

"Are you done with the wise-guy routine?" she asks, and I glimpse the spaces where she's missing teeth.

It ain't from some accident. Someone's tortured this woman, used her flesh like a canvas.

I nod. Definitely done. "You are?"

"That can wait. You'll understand why. I want you to hear me out first."

I glance at my computer screen. An email from a source in the Haven Police Department is open, my most recent care package of cold cases and unexplainable shit from the HPD archives. I still have some contacts that send cases my way, ones that are just too odd to spend manpower on.

Ain't all roses, though. There's more than a few folk on the force who are nothing but a serious pain in my ass.

Something about this woman tickles my mind. Grabbing the bottle of Jack Daniels, I refill my glass and pour some into another for her. She offers me a slight smile, scars pulling tighter, and takes a sip.

"How can I help you?" I ask, holding the tumbler in my hand, without drinking.

I've found over the years other people unwind if it looks like I'm joining them, and this woman looks like she could do with a little something. So I hold it and I let her drink. Don't wanna get loaded.

Even if it is my anniversary.

"Someone is following me," she replies, in an even tone. She tosses her hood back and her hair, thick and lustrous, spills out in a wave of chocolate running down to her waist.

"Don't take those sorts of cases anymore," I say. I reach for a cigarette but have second thoughts. Smoking can wait.

For now. "Tried the police?"

"I can't do that," she replies, puckered lips twitching.

There's something here, beneath the surface, that's pulling at me. It makes the hair on the back of my neck bristle under my collar. I don't get walk-ins often—I mostly work referrals now—and when I do I tend to turn them down. The ones who seek me out are looking for something I can't give them.

There are people who work those mundane cases but, far as I can tell, I'm the only one who specializes in the paranormal. HPD turns to me when they've exhausted their possibilities, not that the boys at the precinct call them paranormal cases. I haven't worked a straight case since the guy I got paid to tail left three holes in my chest and left me for dead. But...

"Any idea why someone would want to follow you?"

She takes another sip.

"I could think of a dozen reasons, but that doesn't concern me. It's the 'who' that bothers me."

"Wait," I say, leaning back in my chair. "You're not 'concerned' about being followed?"

"No." She gives me that tight smile again. "It's expected. I've always been careful, and I can see the signs. A bad tail is good company, they say. But not this time. They follow me everywhere and they followed me here too."

I roll my eyes and spin my chair, taking a glance out the window. I should be used to riddles by now. For a guy who works with ghosts and demons, I get my share of cryptic answers. Some of the folks I've met make spirit boards look eloquent.

Below, on the sidewalk, a man stares at my window

with no pretense.

"Well, I'll be damned," I mutter, turning back to her and throwing a thumb over my shoulder. "Looks like you were right. There's your stalker, out on the street. Either he got sloppy, or you forgot 'the signs.'"

She springs to her feet and strides to the window, gripping the ledge and narrowing her eyes. I watch her sweep the sidewalk, straight past the guy I pointed out.

"Where?" she bites out. "I don't see him."

"There," I reply, pointing down at the figure.

Then I realize my mistake.

The rain doesn't trouble him. Instead, it appears to fall around and through him. I squint. Can't make out his face—the haze of rain and distance obscure it—but his skin and the clothes he's wearing look drained of color, like cheap fabric washed one too many times. If I had a swatch, I'd call his shade 'Darcy'.

The woman returns to her seat and crosses her legs, looking like the cat that got the cream and a little extra on top. The look of triumph on her face doesn't match the scar tissue all over.

"So, what I've heard about you is true," she says.

It's my turn to take a drink. "Who do you think's following you?" I ask, tapping a finger against my desk, frustrated at the ruse.

She coulda just asked if I were legit.

"My husband."

"When did he die?"

"Four weeks ago," she replies, without a hint of grief, "and he's been trailing me ever since. I didn't notice him the first week, just a chill. You know that feeling you get when someone stares at you? Then the presence grew. I can't explain it, but I sense him everywhere. It terrifies me."

Silence falls, except for the pitter-patter against my window. A thought batters against my brain, but I don't want to listen to it.

"Huh," I breathe, just to say something. I know there's a question I should ask, but my tongue knots up and refuses.

"Is it true what they say? That spirits remain when they have unfinished business?"

She motions at her glass with a gnarled finger, interested in both kinds of spirits. I refill it. Mine too.

"Kinda."

My admiration of this woman increases with my intrigue and they combine to swat away my anger. She's done her research and having her suspicions confirmed doesn't make her panic, even for a moment. Even so, I can tell by the tightness around her eyes it's a facade. She's scared.

Still, she'd make a Hell of a P.I. and a damn good poker player.

"They stick around if they have a purpose, but once the purpose is done, they fade. Others need to be forced to fade, if they've turned malevolent. And then there are the ones who just...hang around."

"Ask your question, Mr. Holleran. I can see it on the tip of your tongue."

"What's your name?" I ask, and I can feel three blooms of pain burning in my chest.

He died four weeks ago. The man who killed me.

"My name is Michelle Wheeler."

"Wheeler?" I ask. The bullet wounds pin me to the back of my chair.

"Yes, my husband is Dean Wheeler."

It's five years ago and I'm staring into that alley again, deciding on my next move. Dean Wheeler headed in here and he hasn't come back out. A voice inside tells me it's a bad idea to follow him; another reminds me I'm due a payday. Like an idiot, I listen to the second one and I strut right on in. Only it's a dead end.

I turn, and there he is, gun leveled at me. Safety off, hammer cocked. My stomach lurches. I'm shit outta luck.

"Who hired you?" he asks, taking a step forward.

"Don't know what you're talking about," I reply, holding my hands above my head. "I came down here to take a leak."

Once again, money has made an asshole out of me. My clients offered me hard cash for photos of Wheeler's every movement, so long as I got them quick. Haste makes sloppy work.

"Last mistake you'll ever make, friend."

Wheeler pulls the trigger and the muzzle flashes. The gunshot echoes through the alley before he even finishes his sentence. I glance down and see the blood spreading across my white shirt. I'm aware it's ruined now. I taste iron, but I feel no pain.

Another gunshot comes less than a second later, and my body jolts with the impact. The agony is instant this time and I fall onto my back in the garbage.

Tears trickle from my eyes and I thank God it's a clear night. I can see the stars. Wheeler stands over me and smiles.

He aims the gun at my chest and fires a third time.

Michelle Wheeler watches me, the tumbler of Jack held to her lips. I never saw the woman when I worked the Wheeler case, though I heard her name. A simple job, or so I thought. I'd cut corners and paid the ultimate price.

Or I would have, if it hadn't been for Rosa—the woman who'd held the blood inside me, who'd dialed 911. I haven't spoken to her in too long. Guilt rises, and I snarl inside as I shove it back where it came from.

I turn to my window. The ghost's face is clear now. Dean Wheeler's vacant eyes peer up at me. Fear whispers to me. He's there, staring at me. The man who killed me.

I catch myself, shake my head, throwing the memories out and pulling my thoughts back to the matter at hand.

"You know your husband shot me?" I ask.

It isn't a well-known fact. When I regained consciousness, I told the cops it'd been a mugging gone wrong. Dean Wheeler had his fingers in Haven's organized crime. In deep. Even in the state Wheeler had left me in, my employers, a rival crime family, wouldn't have wanted me blabbing.

They sent me a bottle of twenty-year-old whisky, a bouquet, and a ten-thousand-dollar check for services rendered. I haven't cashed it. Drank the whisky though.

Wheeler never tried to finish me off. Guess I never mattered much to him. The bug crushed underfoot; he knew I wouldn't talk. I'll admit, revenge crossed my mind, but it's a sin. I've seen Heaven, or at least a glimpse of it, and I want a place there when I pass.

"He shot a lot of people," she replied, placing the glass on my desk. "And he always got away with it. You see why

I ruled out the police, other than the fact they wouldn't believe him, or be able to stop him? I need you to find out why his ghost is following me. Can you do it?"

"Depends," I reply, looking out of the window while I consider my next words.

I half-expect to see Dean Wheeler looming behind me in the reflection. He isn't there, and his spirit's vanished from the sidewalk. Some dead are aware straight away; others grow into it. Looks like Wheeler is Strengthening, able to understand what he is and act on his own. And that ain't good.

"Why would your husband want to haunt you?"

"Let's see." Michelle leans forward and places her twisted hands on the desk in front of me. Exhibit A. "He tortured me, and worse. He needed to possess me in life. My husband's brutality terrified me, and I wasn't the only one. Why would it be any different now that he's dead? You of all people should know that, sometimes, death doesn't change anything."

She waits for an answer, staring with such intense heat. I give two fucks to politeness and pull out a cigarette, taking my time to light it. That first drag is exquisite, like a rush of hot silk into my lungs. That sweet fucking nicotine halts the tremble in my fingers as it hits my bloodstream. I feel warm. Steady. Clear. I shut my eyes and let the smoke linger in my mouth just a little. I let it curl out of me and it trails my upper lip like a loving fingertip.

"Listen," I say, watching the smoke tie a grey ribbon around the ceiling fan. "This could get worse. If he's hurt you before, you could be his unfinished business. Dean could stay a regular ghost—harmless. But, if he Strengthens, meaning his personality returns and he can affect the living, you're not safe. If you're right, that possessing you is the end goal, there's only one way he gets to do that, and that's if you're there with him in the afterlife. We can't let that happen."

I'm surprised at my fervor. I can't get the image of Dean gunning me down out of my head, and this damaged, but unbroken, woman in front of me is galvanizing the anger I thought I'd put to bed.

"There's no time, is what you're saying," she says, biting her torn lip. "Will you help me?"

"That's not even the question. I'll help you, but we'll have to work fast. Wheeler may be here for another reason and I have to find what that is. There are ways I can convince him to leave but that's messy, and it's a last resort. Either way, I'm going to need materials that aren't easy to come by."

Haste makes sloppy work, Nick.

Yeah, and dragging our feet is going to make us both corpses.

"Money isn't an issue," she breathes.

I notice her shoulders droop as the tension leaves her body. She's convinced me now. Hard part's over. Still, there's more to this case than she's letting on. I'm just finding it hard to care. All I see is Wheeler, gunning me down in that alley.

"It is for some, sweetheart," I say, sliding over a piece of card and a pen. "I've another client due, but leave me your cell. I'll have more questions for you. Where can I find you?"

Michelle pinches the pen in four fingers—articulating

her mutilated hands like claws—and scrawls her number, then passes it across to me. She holds my stare again.

Those shining eyes.

"Home. I've nowhere else to go. I'll speak with you soon, Mister Holleran."

She takes my card from the stack on the desk and leaves without a backward glance. I stare out the window, smoking my cigarette. I see her stride down the sidewalk, hood, mask and gloves back in place.

Darcy and I are alone again. She didn't stop staring at the wall for even a moment. Does she listen to my conversations? Can she even hear them? Does she care what goes on beyond that space?

I don't have another client coming. I wanted Michelle to leave so that I can plan. I've said I'll take the case. It should buy me a day or two's grace so I can investigate Dean Wheeler's death myself.

Even without what he did to her, how could I turn it down? It's personal.

TROUBLE AT THE STYX

Reaching out to my sources unearths information. Police ruled Wheeler's death a suicide, but the crew Dean ran with don't believe it. Michelle Wheeler is a person of interest and the local PD is keeping tabs.

They like to keep an eye on me too. In particular, Detectives Henry Butler and Lori Gavin. They never liked me when I took regular P.I. work from the department. Now that I show up in the unlikeliest of places with no credible reason for being there, it's gone from professional distaste to outright suspicion.

From time to time, they come by my office to shake me down, but I know my rights and I still have friends. It pisses them off but, I have to admit, it amuses me. And in Hell, I'll take my kicks where I can get 'em.

Still, no one likes being followed by paranoid cops.

Then there's the matter of Dean Wheeler.

What does the dead sonofabitch want? Spirits manifest in unique ways, but they all start the same way. There's some instinct that drives them. In Wheeler's case, it seems to be stalking his wife. Some ghosts stay like that—living a half-forgotten echo of their life—like Darcy. Others

Strengthen, and that can get interesting. They accept their new existence and enjoy the liberation death grants them. I know one or two.

Not that the liberation of death is good for everyone. Some folks come back angry and hateful, maybe because they were in life.

Wheeler strikes me as the angry and hateful type, and they need dealing with. The sooner, the better.

Malevolent ghosts can exert their will on Hell, interact with it just like the living can. I mean, they live here, right? Why shouldn't they?

Ghosts can touch things to varying degrees, depending on their will, their fortitude. The longer they exist in Hell, the easier it gets for them, but those that Strengthen early and have nefarious purposes can cause all kinds of goddamned trouble.

And let me tell you, ghosts are the least of the entities I worry about round here.

Going outside is something I hated doing after I died. It took a lot of getting used to. I'd walk with my eyes down, shoulders slumped and narrow, avoiding the living and the dead. Now, the scenes are as familiar to me as the bullet wounds in my chest. Leaving my office, I stroll past the washed-out figure of a man with a long beard in shirtsleeves and braces. He kneels, staring at the palms of his hands, and weeps. A specter from another era, locked in grief since I first laid eyes on him five years ago, and only God knows how long he's been there.

Well, maybe Satan does too. We're all down here in his joint.

Ghosts come and go. It depends on how present they are. The fact Wheeler vanished from the sidewalk is the first sign of both Awareness and Strengthening.

It's normal for them to leave the living to themselves, even the ghosts who are Aware. There are exceptions of course; there always are. One guy I know, Eddy, died in 1927. He doesn't remember why he stuck around, though from the stories he tells, I reckon he enjoyed a straight flush of sins. Nice fella, checks in on his family line once a week. None of them lived when he walked the earth, but it's a gracious gesture all the same.

I make my way to the Styx Bar. Place is a dive, but the goths love it; black wallpaper, black carpets, and apathy on tap. The owner, Ruby, is like me. She died for four minutes as a child, swallowed something she shouldn't have and choked. Course, her old man brought her back, and she's lived knowing the truth ever since.

Almost sixty goddamn years. And I think five's been a burden.

I learned a lot from Ruby, and from the Styx. Most of Haven's sentient supernatural know it as a place for the weird and wonderful denizens of the Underworld to hang out together, swap news and stories and have a good time. Hell, I like the place. Ruby split the joint into two floors before I was even born. Upstairs for the living, a classic dive that doesn't attract a lot of patrons. The real business is downstairs, where the dead, the demons and other denizens lurk. *The Tomb of Nick Cage* are the house band, and the basement customers are, for the most part, my kind of people. Dead people.

The damp Fall heat dogs my steps, and I'm glad to get inside the Styx with its air conditioning, a fact that staggered me the first time I entered. It doesn't look like the kind of place that's even *heard* of air con. More than once over the years, I've thanked my lucky stars Ruby reached out to me. She keeps her ear to the ground for news, and a bar is a prime location to build a network.

I still remember the email that landed in my inbox one afternoon: 'Mr. Holleran, meet me at the Styx. You're gonna get yourself killed. Again.'

I laughed it off at the time, but I never deleted it. Just kept reading it until the day I decided I needed to know more. That damned curiosity again.

Let's just say, knowing Ruby has kept me living my second life. She gives good advice. Direct, but sound. And she doesn't suffer fools.

Four or five people are sitting with bottled beer as an angst-ridden teenager plays acoustic guitar on stage, dyed raven hair falling like curtains over his forehead. I smile at the sight of one of the Styx's resident demons, Cyril, sitting in rapt attention. He's immense, his muscled bulk covered in red and purple scales. His lower teeth protrude from his jaw like tusks. If the human patrons of the bar knew Cyril—I don't know who named him—sat amongst them, they'd run a mile. And then keep running for one or two more.

See, the living don't see his kind at all. It's like their minds don't comprehend demons and the like. Their eyes just slide over them. The chair Cyril sits in would stay 'empty' all night, and no one would mention it. No one would even try to sit at his table. It's like some subconscious self-preservation instinct. A demon wouldn't react well to some human sitting in its lap.

Sometimes, I think the living do know on some level; I remember the times I'd get goosebumps or feel anxious for no reason at all. You know that old saying when you'd shiver on a roasting day? 'Someone's stepped on my grave.' That didn't happen, but maybe a demon took a seat next to you on a bus.

The smile fades from my face as I remember something else. Cyril's the reason I ain't called into the Styx for a while. I lower my head and take a couple of steps back, hoping the Robert Smith-wannabe on stage keeps the demon's attention.

Nodding at Guz, the barman, I step behind the bar and through a door with a sign that reads: STAFF ONLY. It ain't really for people who work at the Styx. It leads downstairs, and it's the place for dead-friendly folk like me and the rest of Hell.

What I grew to understand is that the demons, ghosts and all the creatures of Hell have existed thousands of years. And these folk, just like humans, have their vices. They eat, drink, shit and curse like the rest of us. Ghosts even have their own liquor. Tasted it once. It's like paint stripper. Felt it tearing up my insides as I gulped it down. Never again, let me tell you.

Not all of them can drink right away. It takes concentration and will to hold a glass. But once they learn, they drink. Why the Hell not?

They have their own society, their own laws—I've worked more than one case on behalf of demon kind in the last five years—and just like humans, there are demons and ghosts I like. And there are assholes. Cyril is the former, but I'm thankful to avoid him as I slink down the stairs to Styx proper—me and his ex, Francis, disagreed a while back, and it didn't end well for Francis. Sometimes jobs just go that way.

Ruby's behind the bar, wiping down while she chats to some washed-out stiff. She sees me and her eyes narrow. Nice, just the reaction I like to get from people.

The joint isn't busy. Two Strengthened ghosts I don't recognize are talking by the jukebox—*Helter Skelter* by The Beatles is playing, which I'm sure would give old Charlie Manson a giggle—and, much to my delight, a Nephilim sits at the bar, nursing a bottle of Scotch.

Nephilim are an enormous deal, highest on the hierarchy of Hell, just below Lucifer himself and no one ever sees him. The children of angels and the daughters of men, they've been around since the Eden days. So Sunday School used to preach. Only they weren't wiped out like we were told. God granted them clemency and, in return, the Nephilim sided with their fathers against Heaven. And, when their commander-in-chief fell, the gates closed to them forever. My buddy, Harry tells me the Bible had the story mostly right, and he's read up on a lot of lore in his time.

Always a touch of truth in legends, my boy, he says.

I should check in with him and Maeve; it's been too long.

It's part of my mission to discover the truth. A Nephilim would be an ideal next step, but they don't talk much. Haven's home to two of them, and this one's name is Suraz.

I've exchanged nods with him, and I've only ever glimpsed the other. Her name's Absin and she keeps to herself for the most part.

They're the saddest creatures I've ever laid eyes on, and seeing as we're all living in Hell, that's saying something.

Suraz's raven hair flows to his waist above his gold-plated armor, and his skin is the same color as his hair, like obsidian. Strapped to his back is a golden sword, about six feet in length. The sight of it's enough to make most folk in Hell fall into line if they're acting a little rowdy.

It should. I mean, imagine getting impaled by that thing.

I take a seat a few stools down. He glances at me. His deep yellow eyes hold eons-worth of sorrow. I nod and he inclines his head, then turns back to his bottle. Like I said, everyone in Hell has their vices. Suraz has seen Heaven, and can never return. No wonder he's drinking.

Rosa used to say I held too much sadness in my blue eyes for her to stand. That seems a long time ago now. A wave of longing rises in my guts. My thoughts often turn to Rosa when I least expect it.

If anyone would know the answers to the questions that plague me—Hell on Earth and why—a Nephilim would know. They've been around since the beginning, spoken to everyone from the top to the bottom. Problem is, they don't do a lot of talking. And when they do, it's not to answer questions from the likes of me.

Still, I might have something Suraz wants. I saw Heaven, just five years ago. Felt its glow. Maybe we can trade, a story for a story. A little glimpse of what he's been craving all this time. I just don't know how the Hell I'm going to articulate the sensation of going to paradise.

"Holleran," Ruby says, breaking my concentration. She's frowning at me now. She'd been gazing at Suraz until a second ago. Easy to understand; a Nephilim's beauty surpasses all else. "Cyril's upstairs. I'm sure you noticed. Is there going to be trouble?"

I spread my hands and give her my best grin. Lopsided and boyish, I'm told. "Me? Come on, Rubes. You know I ain't like that. He didn't see me come in. American Goth Idol upstairs has his attention for the night. I just need some info, that's all. And a drink?"

She cocks her head, raises an eyebrow. Ever the skeptic. "Right. Long time, no see. What can I get ya?"

"Coffee, please," I reply, slipping my jacket off. "So. What's new?"

"Plenty. Wendigo sightings out in the country. Notice how the sky seems darker at night than it used to? Red during the day too. Something's in the air, Holleran."

I nod in agreement as she moves to the coffee machine. She's tall, about five-ten, with bright pink hair at odds with the deep wrinkles around her eyes and on her forehead. Ruby pulls it off, though. She's what I imagine a sixty-six-year-old PJ Harvey would look like. I take another glance at Suraz. His unfocused stare into the bottom of his bottle suggests he's in a different time zone. Or a different reality.

"Working a fresh case?" Ruby asks, placing black coffee in front of me.

"Maybe," I say. "What've you heard about Dean

Wheeler's death?"

"Wheeler? That crook who shot you?"

I nod. I sense Suraz shift. Out of the corner of my eye, I can see him watching me. Guess he wasn't as far away as I thought.

"Yeah, the one and fucking only. Heard he died four weeks back but tried to ignore it. Water under the bridge, right? His widow came to me today, said her dead husband was stalking her from beyond the grave, that he followed her to my office. She wasn't wrong either. I saw his spirit out in the street. Hasn't Strengthened yet, but you can bet this whole joint he will, and the cocksucker will be trouble."

"Wait," Ruby says, holding her hands up. "How'd she know Wheeler trailed her to your place? Could she see him?"

I do a double-take. The ghosts of my past with Wheeler had clouded my thought process. How *had* Michelle Wheeler known?

"That's a damn good question," I say. "I mean, she said she could *sense* him. She'd done her research so I didn't think much of it. You think she could see him?"

I don't find out what Ruby thinks. She's staring beyond me, her mouth making a perfect O shape.

Shit.

Sulfurous breath smothers me as an iron grip seizes my collar and lifts me into the air. I fly into the far wall and hit the ground hard. The impact against the concrete breaks at least one rib and I fight to breathe as the vice closes around my lungs. Before I realize what's happening, I'm picked up again and pressed against the wall.

Cyril's four eyes, black and glinting, are inches from mine. His furious, brimstone-tainted breath fills my nostrils. He holds me with one hand, and presses the claws of his other into the stubble on my neck.

"Cyril," I say. "Listen, I'm sorry about..."

"Shut the fuck up," the demon barks, his voice a mixture of rage and grief. "Don't you even say his name."

I hoped he wouldn't see me. A fool's fucking hope. Like I said, Cyril was the reason I hadn't darkened the Styx's door for a while.

See, Francis and Cyril were familiars. Not lovers like in human terms. It's deeper than that. They mate for all of existence, and demons live a Hell of a long time. They connect on every level—physical, mental, spiritual. They know each other's thoughts, each other's pain. It's a bond too visceral for a human to understand.

A few months back, my source at the local PD passed me a missing persons case that had gone cold. Five missing persons, to be exact. All girls, all sixteen years old, all from the Greater Haven area, and all reported missing on a full moon night.

Turned out old Francis had sacrificed them, looking for a way to speak to Lucifer himself. Harry tells me it's possible, but neither of us have ever come across a soul who's done it. Satan keeps to himself.

Blood sacrifice is nasty business. By the time I found Francis, it was too late to save the girl. He'd ripped her to pieces. Only bits and blood remained. I did what I had to do. Cyril would have felt Francis' destruction. Felt it deep.

"Had no choice, Cyril," I snarl, inching my fingers

towards the Ruger-57 at my waist. Normal bullets wouldn't do much against a demon, but the ones doused with holy water in my magazine would pack a punch. "He murdered five girls. The bloodlust had him. He'd have ripped me limb-from-limb. I know you don't want to hear that, but Francis forced my hand. I had to Expunge him."

I'm right. It isn't what he wants to hear. He wants his partner back. Failing that, he wants to watch me bleed. With a growl, he draws his claws back, ready to tear my throat out.

"Stop."

It's like a whisper, but the command reverberates inside my head, almost to the point of pain. My fingers had already found the revolver's handle, but they stay there, unable to move. I look past Cyril and see my savior, Suraz, standing as tall as the monster holding me. His golden eyes burn into mine, his mighty sword gripped in both hands, point scraping the tiles on the floor. My instincts scream at me, tell me to look away, but I can't. Suraz's focus is like a force of nature. Stronger, even.

"Is this true, demon?" he asks, soft voice hard as titanium.

Cyril snarls, but has no choice but to answer. The Nephilim's will forces him to speak. When Suraz and his kind want to know something, only Lucifer himself can withstand them. And maybe Charon, that sonofabitch.

"Yes," he bites out, saliva dripping from his maw. "But Expunging? He's gone, Suraz. Forever."

For a moment, I pity the demon. I could never comprehend his loss. Expunging wipes a creature from existence. It doesn't work on humans, but makes a ghost or demon vanish, with no chance of returning.

It's not something I enjoy doing, but it's an ace in the hole. When I Expunged Francis, Cyril would have felt his partner's confusion, his fear as he stared into oblivion. Then...nothing.

Where his bond with Francis once lived, emptiness would have replaced it.

My empathy ends as, with a snarl, the demon takes a swipe at me.

Suraz is faster. Like a blur, he drives his golden blade into the demon's back and through his chest. Ichor spatters my blond hair, streaking it black and stinking of sulfur. Cyril's grip loosens, and I slide to the floor. The demon copies me and, a second later, his decapitated head bounces off the tiles, tongue lolling between his tusks and lifeless eyes staring toward Heaven.

"Some advice, human," Suraz murmurs, his whispers beating at my skull. "You play a dangerous game in our world, but I see in your eyes you cannot stop yourself. Tread with care. Ruby is correct. Something is amiss, and it troubles me."

With that, the Nephilim turns and strides for the exit. I look at Ruby over Cyril's perforated corpse. She sighs and points at the body.

"Jesus fucking Christ, Nick, I thought you said you wouldn't cause any trouble. You just got my best customer killed."

"I thought *I* was your best customer."

She considers for a moment. "Tell you what. Help me clean up this mess and I'll think about it."

ILL OMENS

Cleaning up after a Nephilim impales, then decapitates, a demon of Hell is just as fun as it sounds.

"So, Dean Wheeler..." Ruby says. I grunt in reply.

We've talked only a little since Suraz made Cyril a head shorter. Thick, black blood stains the floorboards, and I'm covered in it. Its sulfurous smell lingers, like someone's pushing a finger down my throat. Ichor crusting into my hair and skin is not a pleasant sensation.

"Yeah," I say, hoping that speaking might distract my nose. "Dean fucking Wheeler. You know the story. Five years back, I had a job to trail him. Didn't get much from him, except three to the chest. Tried to forget about the sonofabitch after that. You know anything I don't?"

Ruby stands with a sigh and rolls her neck, working her shoulders. "This fucking blood'll stain for weeks," she says, tossing her mop into the filth-encrusted bucket. "I've probably heard what everyone else has heard about Wheeler. The family's notorious, Dean in particular. Drugs, guns, girls. Hard to find items. Reckon they knew him as far as Seattle but that's neither here nor there. What'll concern *you* is, two or three years back, he came snooping around upstairs, bothering Guz about some 'secret' bar for 'certain' types of customers. 'VIPs' he kept calling them. I dug a little. Always do when people come by asking questions. Word is, Dean Wheeler took an interest in the supernatural. Now, they say suicide finished him, but a piece of work like that taking his own life? No, I'm not buying it. Not a chance."

"This is getting too fucking interesting," I mutter, reaching for a cigarette. I tried vaping after I died for a while, but what's the point? Not going to get me to Heaven any quicker. "I guess it makes sense. Someone must have clued Michelle in on our world. I mean, there's plenty of folk out there who believe in spirits, creatures and things, right? But she did her homework after she suspected her dead husband started following her, and when I confirmed it, she wasn't surprised. Not by a long shot. She fucking knew about Hell, and here's me, too wrapped up in Dean goddamn Wheeler to notice. Doesn't change a thing though. It's been weeks, so Wheeler's spirit is still working on instinct, but if he's following her already, I don't think I want to leave it till he Strengthens to find out what his unfinished business is."

"That leaves the wife as your lead," Ruby says, with a nod.

"Yes, it does," I drawl. "She knows more than she's letting on. My guys tell me the cops and Wheeler's old associates are watching her too. Think I need to pay her a visit. Plus, wherever she is, her husband won't be far behind. Need me to stay and help some more?"

Ruby laughs. It's a sound full of heart. She always looks on the bright side of Hell. "Go. You've not done much more than spread poor Cyril's blood around the place. Going to miss that guy, but that's life, right?"

I stand with a grimace that's almost a smile and retrieve my jacket. Ruby calls after me as I head for the stairs. "Nick? If the state of Hell worries a Nephilim, I'd be extra careful out there. Something has him spooked."

Spooked. Good one.

"Hey, it's me. I'm always careful." She rolls her eyes. Fair response, all things considered. "Thanks, Ruby. See ya around."

Throwing her a wink, I leave the Styx. It's time to find out what in Hell is going on.

...

My smartphone tells me it's just past 10 p.m. Michelle Wheeler should be at home, and lucky for me I know where that is. I staked the place out once or twice before dying in that alley—an enormous mansion on the outskirts of Haven—but intuition tells me I'm going to need to prepare before I head over there.

Ruby's right: If a Nephilim's worried, we should all be worried.

I have Michelle's number. It'd be easy to call her, but I want to look into those beautiful eyes of hers when she lies to me again. It's a fetish of mine.

Two million people live in Haven and there might be even more dead. With a population that size, there's a good number of folk who've had experiences like me and Ruby. Some get jobs as psychics and mediums. Sad part is, they have to try not to be too accurate because that's how witch hunts get started.

There's cults too, and plenty of them. Without the guidance of folks like Ruby and Harry, some people have their own interpretation of this big, old underworld we're living in and they can get pretty out there. Not that I blame them. There's a lot going on down here that's not easy to understand.

And then there's the devil worshippers. Freaks. I try to steer clear when I can.

Regular folk stumble across the truth from time to time, and there's some whose families discover the truth about Hell and pass the information on, making it their mission to learn what they can. The latter's who I need to confer with, and I know just the people—Harry and Maeve.

I flag down a passing taxi and climb in, murmur the address I want, and let my thoughts drift to the Wheelers. It bothers me that Dean's dead. Part of me wanted to be the one to kill him. That road would have led to too much heat, and now I know Heaven's real, I want to save my place. Killing Wheeler would be wrathful, and that's one of the Seven Deadly right there.

My excitement at the prospect of Expunging him, like I did with Francis, worries me even more. I need to be sure I'm righteous when I do it, or I'm just a murderer like they are. Worse, because I'm eradicating them from existence. At least the girls Francis killed can move on, just like I should've.

Might seem strange, planning to kill a ghost, but it can be done. Expunging isn't about the body or the blood or the heart. It's about the essence and the soul. Anything in Hell can be Expunged.

I know I'm not above the desire for revenge—I've

fantasized about it long and often—but Expunging is more than that.

Picture the universe as a rug, made up of a multitude of cotton threads of equal importance. Every person in Hell, alive or not, is a thread. Expunging someone unravels them entirely, stops them from ascending to Heaven or remaining in Hell. Sometimes, it's necessary, but do it too much and holes start to appear. The fabric wears thin and, before you know it, the rug tears apart completely.

I don't imagine the big bastard upstairs or his friend down here would be too happy about me ruining their carpet. And look, despite appearances, I got a conscience. I've looked into the Expunged's eyes when they realize what's happening to them. They've peered into oblivion, the endless void staring back, and they understand there's nowhere to run.

That kind of expression haunts a guy.

...

The cab pulls up on Norris Street, where Harry and Maeve live. It's in a sleepy part of Haven. Idyllic really, if it weren't for a handful of shades roaming around, reminding me I'm in Hell.

I linger outside as I stare at a name and number on my smartphone: Rosa's.

On the way over, my thoughts drifted to her, as they often do. The stranger who stopped to save a dying man. We became close after, but it didn't work out. I'd have ascended to Heaven if it weren't for her and I couldn't just forget that.

Everywhere we went together, I saw the ghosts and demons and knew I wouldn't be seeing any of it if she'd just kept walking.

She never gave up on me. Not that night in the alley and not after, like she was still trying to keep me from bleeding out. I couldn't leave that open wound alone, got personal with it, asked her who she'd lost that *I'd* become the one she needed to save.

I think her last words to me were, "That's bullshit, Nick. Call me when you're ready to wise up."

I never did call.

Rosa knows the truth; I told her everything. The cell phone's heavy in my hand and the old bullet wounds itch beneath my shirt. I stare at the photo on her profile. Damn, I remember taking it myself. Feels like yesterday, or like years ago, that we were solid. Then I fucked things up again, pushed her away, grew distant, threw myself into cold cases just as things started to heat up between us.

No doubt about it. I'm a grade-A schmuck.

Well, no time like the present to make amends. Not when the past has already walked itself right to my door. I press the call button, though it's more like a stab as I change my mind mid-action and my finger lurches forward. The coward inside me hangs up, but not fast enough. My phone vibrates. Rosa, calling back.

"Nick?" I hear her voice, filled with concern, as I press the phone to my ear.

"Hey, Rosa, sorry. Must have pocket-dialed you."

A beat of silence.

"Right... Answered pretty quick for a pocket dial.

Well, nice hearing from you, Nick."

"Wait," I say, with a little too much desperation. "That's a lie. Guess I wanted to hear your voice, is all."

"Nick, what's going on? I haven't heard from you in about a year. Now you're lying about calling me at 10:30 on a Friday night? Are you drunk?"

I laugh, but it's a little strained.

"Sorry, I wasn't thinking. Not sure I even knew what time it was." I pause. I can hear her breathing and the soft murmur of her TV playing in the background. I bite the bullet. "Listen, Dean Wheeler's dead."

"Good," she replies with heat.

"That's not all. His widow wants me to work for her. She says he's following her around, but something doesn't feel right."

"You think?" I can picture her head shaking at my dumbness, dark skin creasing into a frown around those features I came to adore. "That's a little coincidental, don't you think? I know that scumbag wouldn't let death stop him from being a creep, but are you sure you're not getting played?"

The air's gone cold in a matter of seconds, and I can see my breath fogging in the air. I glance around but see nothing. I'm alone in the deserted street. The ghosts that lingered here moments ago have vanished.

"No," I say. "But you shoulda seen his wife. He did awful, disgusting things to her, Rosa. I don't want more blood on my hands if I can help it."

"Nick, is this about revenge? Because if it is... Well, you know better than that. I hope."

A shiver runs through my body. Not at Rosa's words—

I've been pondering them myself—but at the cold. Frost glints on the sidewalk beneath my feet. This ain't natural. Not by a long shot.

There's an aggressive absence of sound, making Rosa's breathing so loud it beats at my skull. I detect the stench of animal musk in the air and something else. Trouble.

"Look Rosa, I gotta go," I say.

Her garbled voice chops in and out in my ear until my phone beeps and the call drops. No service. Shit.

Mist oozes from the asphalt, and the trouble I sniffed before is pungent.

Drawing my Ruger helps my stomach unclench, but I know I'm under-prepared. I think of my survival kit, sat in my office, and I'd chide myself if I thought I could get a word out without choking. Have to admit, I've not kept on top of my supplies recently. Getting sloppy.

My consecrated bullets will only work against certain Hellspawn, and as I recount every demon, devil and device that could cause instantaneous winter, a figure padding out of the fog confirms my worst fears.

I fucking hate Amaroks.

Fast, powerful, intelligent and far too wicked for my tastes. Picture a wolf, but more. Thick muscle hulks beneath its silver fur as it pads on all fours through the mist, keen eyes fixed on me. Parts of it glitters as the moonlight catches the shards of ice protruding from its spine and shoulder blades, like freezing-sharp armor. They say the best offense is a good defense, right?

Yeah, Amaroks love the colder parts of Hell, but they tend to bring the weather with them. Its red eyes glint at me through the gloom. Saliva drips from its razor-sharp fangs. It sizzles when it hits the floor.

There's a plus side. Unlike normal wolves, an Amarok hunts alone. Not that I'm thanking my lucky stars just yet. This beast is still the size of a small pony.

It begs the question: What the hell does it want with me? As far as I know, I've done nothing to piss off an Amarok for some time. Learned my lesson the hard way.

"Well, shit," I mutter, as I pull out what might be my last cigarette. It isn't just for pleasure. Amaroks hate fire, and though the amount my lighter emits is small, it's all I've got. "Mind if I finish this?"

The Amarok howls, saliva shooting from its maw, sizzling where it lands. Its cry curdles my blood, makes it twist in my veins. I wanna turn, run into the night, but I know the Amarok will chase me down, sink its claws and teeth into my spine. Instead, I grind my teeth and try to stop my legs turning to jelly.

You know that sensation when you wake in the middle of the night startled and afraid, but you don't know why? That's one of these bastards howling close by. A normal human doesn't hear it, but on some level they *feel* it. Well, right now, I'm facing the full brunt.

As the cry dies down, another answers, and it's too close for comfort. I spin around and, sitting twenty feet behind me, is another goddamn Amarok. Maybe it's a trick of the light, but I think it's smiling at me.

"Well, fuck me."

I take one last, sweet lungful of my cigarette, sucking back on that fucker because I need to get my money's worth, then toss it to the ground. I hold my lighter like a shield, forcing back one Amarok, and aim my revolver at the other.

Realization floods in. I'm shit outta luck, and that ember, dying on the ground, is the last nicotine I'll ever fucking inhale.

"The One Who Wheels sends their regards," the newcomer growls, the words awkward in its maw.

I've no time to think. The wolf to my left lets out a snarl and pounces. Leaping back, I swing my aim around and pull the trigger, fighting the urge to keep firing. There's only so many bullets. The Amarok changes direction midair to avoid being hit and lands with a gymnast's grace on four legs. Bastard's fast.

Despite the cold, I tear off my jacket, a plan forming. I seize the hip flask in my inner pocket and douse my favorite coat, the one that's been with me through thick and thin. It's just the latest in a long line of things Wheeler's taken from me. I hold the lighter to the dripping fabric and the flames burst to life. I throw my makeshift fireball between me and the Hellspawn.

It ignites with speed and I circle it, trying to keep the conflagration between me and the Amaroks. They're intelligent creatures, but their lone-wolf instincts play in my favor. They seem confused at the prospect of working together.

I add to the confusion. I charge at one, lighter in hand, like a desperate Olympic torchbearer gone mad. The thing's the size of a small horse and I've got nothing but a puny fucking lighter. I suppress a giggle at the thought of it. Maybe I really am crazy.

But crazy works. The Amarok scrambles backwards,

and changing direction, I spin and fire at the other. My bullet strikes home, grazing its cheek and embedding itself in the massive wolf's left shoulder, snapping off a shard of ice that melts as soon as it hits the asphalt. It lets out a pained yelp as steam rises from the wound. The holy water's doing its work. The hit won't kill it, but it'll slow it down.

My heart's slamming on my ribs like it's trying to tell me just how much goddamn danger I'm still in, but I'm stood there grinning like an idiot. I let my guard down too long and the other Amarok recovers and pounces onto my back, knocking me aside with a backhanded swipe of its paw. Pain explodes as my face scrapes the ground and my arms shred on the rough asphalt.

Instinct takes over and I roll, keeping as much space between them as I can. As the sizzling pavement shows, an Amarok's saliva alone could burn through my flesh, never mind fangs and claws. I'm lucky they've not landed a good hit on me yet.

It's only a matter of time.

Fuck off.

I'm afraid, sure, but that's nothing new, and I can't give in to it. I won't. Scrambling to my feet, I point the Ruger, ready to fire as soon as I see the reds of the Hellspawn's eyes.

But I've lost my advantage. The injured Amarok sends me spinning as it charges past me, clipping me enough to knock me onto my back, and driving the wind out of me as I crash to the ground again. That cracked rib Cyril left me howls in protest.

I'm having a very bad night.

As my revolver and lighter spin from my grip, as my breath comes in labored gasps, I realize I'm fucked. The Amaroks prowl closer, the flames of my burning jacket dying behind them. I close my eyes, hoping it'll be quick and that Heaven still waits for me. I've lasted longer than I should have against two Amaroks. That same, crazy stubbornness that kept me from ascending the first time.

As I wait for one of the beasts to snap their jaws into my neck, I think of all the things I'll never be able to tell Rosa, and how Michelle Wheeler's helpless against whatever her husband's got planned.

Then a warm glow washes over me, and my eyes snap open. The monstrous wolves shrink back as a figure steps past. I laugh, filled with sudden relief. Perhaps I'm not about to die again just yet. Look, I'm not ready, and the last five minutes has painted that in bright red fucking letters.

"About goddamn time!" I cry.

It's Maeve, a Strengthened ghost. Don't think I mentioned that. Well, right now, I'd be happy to see Lucifer himself so long as he's on my side.

Her presence fills the street, chasing away the Amarok's frost. My oppressors whimper, their mighty tails drooping between the legs. They ain't beaten yet. The injured wolf nips at the other, urging it forward. They're intelligent creatures and know a Strengthened ghost has limits. By rights, a Hellspawn should have the advantage,

The Amarok steps forward.

A projectile tears into it, bursting into flames. The beast howls as its fur burns, cries of rage, of pain. Pathetic whimpers from such a powerful creature, but ones I'm delighted to hear. The stench of cooking, putrid flesh fills the air, followed by the unmistakable stink of shit as its fur singes too. It looks at its partner in desperation as it collapses, bones turning to liquid from the heat, the ice protruding from its flesh melting.

Turns out an Amarok's bones are made from ice too. Who knew?

The monster melts before our eyes. Its partner flees without a backward glance.

I struggle to my feet, my cracked rib keeping me from drawing a full breath, not to mention all the new bumps and scrapes. The burning Amarok is now a steaming puddle of blood, marrow, ice and fur. Maeve watches me, and I nod to her.

"Thanks," I say. "Maybe don't leave it so late next time?"

"Well," Maeve replies, still watching the Amarok with a thoughtful frown. "Call when you're coming over next time. Made enough of a commotion though."

"And we had to prepare the grenade," a voice calls.

It's Harry, Maeve's husband. He's alive, but comes from a long line of 'Truthers'—people who've known about this world for generations—and when they met, he brought Maeve in on the secret too.

Harry's a healthy eighty-seven. He and Maeve died in a car accident back in the 60s. He came back to the land of the living, and she didn't. When Harry woke in his hospital bed, he found Maeve waiting for him, dead but unwilling to move on without him. He blamed himself, being the driver and all, but she wouldn't hear of it.

They helped each other acclimatize to Hell, one living, one dead. Their history as Truthers would have helped, but their bond, stronger than ever, saw them through those early, uncertain years. They're so in love they want to ascend to Heaven together, but Harry still lives his life, and Maeve's by his side, every step of the way.

I envy them, but I'm never happier than when I'm at their place, and that's the truth. I'd bring Rosa here sometimes. Harry and Maeve loved her.

I asked Harry if he ever thought of remarrying, with Maeve's blessing. He said the thought had never entered his mind, and wouldn't speak to me until I apologized for even bringing it up. That's the thing about Truthers. Even death doesn't do them part.

"Much obliged," I mutter, fingers itching and throat dry for another cigarette. I sigh as I remember they were in my jacket.

"Two Amaroks!" Harry cries, slapping me on the shoulder. My rib throbs and I wince. "Unheard of, my boy. A fine battle."

I shake my head, looking around for my Ruger. "No. Way too easy. They shoulda killed me without a struggle. Let's get inside. We need to talk."

OCCULT'S A DIRTY WORD

"Dean Wheeler," Harry says, with a whistle. "If he can bend a pair of Amaroks to his will, four weeks dead, then I'd hate to see what he'll be capable of in another month."

We're sitting inside the old man's study. I've given him and Maeve the blow-by-blow of the day, wincing through the cuts, scrapes, cracked rib and bruises.

I shake my head. So much drama in such a small amount of time. Just hours ago, me and the ghost in my office were reliving my teenage years listening to Nirvana. Now, I've watched as a Nephilim decapitated a demon I didn't even dislike, hit up an ex-flame I ain't spoke to in almost a year and been hunted by a pair of Amarok in the middle of Haven's suburbia.

That's a wild Friday night by anyone's standards.

"What do you think Wheeler wants with you, Nick?" Maeve asks, her translucent stare kind and wise. She's a beautiful ghost, looking the same as she did sixty years ago when she died, despite the washed-out look. From the old photos scattered around the room—one or two in color— she resembled Rita Hayworth; fiery red hair and intelligent brown eyes. Death hasn't dimmed the sharpness of her stare.

"It's obvious he's trying to use you for something. You intend on confronting him?"

I flick my eyes around the room. I love visiting these two. The study alone holds enough books for a library and the house is crammed with Truther curios gathered over a lifetime. The fireplace is a pleasant touch, if careless with all the paper scattered around.

Harry's family researched Hell and its creatures for centuries. The old man continued the tradition, but his line will die with him; Maeve died before they had children. Harry reminds me of Doc Brown from the *Back to the Future* movies. He has the same crazy, white hair and wild look in his eyes. From the way he looks into Maeve's youthful face, I can tell he never gave a second thought about moving on from her. I never really needed to ask.

Still, I'm a curious type. Have to be in my line of work.

"I do," I say, answering Maeve's question. "Best way to disarm a bear trap is just to set it off. I know he's planning something. Ruby at the Styx told me Wheeler's interested in the occult."

"Pah." Maeve would have spat, if she could produce saliva. "That's a dirty word. You know better than that."

I hold up my hands and wince, recognizing my mistake. The denizens of Hell object to the word 'occult'—they say it has negative connotations, and they ain't all bad.

"All right," I say, with my most charming smile, the lopsided one that makes me look boyish and disarming. I think. "Sorry, you know what I mean. He'd researched Hell before he died. And it was more than just morbid curiosity. He came around asking questions, knew more than he should."

"Interesting," Harry muttered, stroking the white stubble on his chin. "Things are strange in Hell. Two Amaroks hunting together is more than enough proof of that. Then you had that unpleasant business with the demon trying to summon Lucifer. Which was utterly ridiculous, I might add. You can't summon the devil with random sacrifices, else he'd appear four times a day across the globe. You need to tap into a specific energy. Cardinal sin. Even the timing has to be right."

"Maybe Francis should have come and talked to you first."

He ignores that. "There's something in the air recently. You've felt it, haven't you, boy? How did Wheeler die?"

"Suicide is the official word."

Harry and Maeve share a glance. It speaks volumes, and I don't like it.

"Shoot," Harry says, getting to his feet. I marvel at how spry he is. "Didn't offer you a drink. Tea, coffee, something stronger?"

"Coffee," I reply, winking at him. "Think it's gonna be a night."

Harry laughs and heads for the kitchen, leaving me alone with his wife. I try to pinpoint when I became so at ease in the presence of the dead but realize it doesn't matter. They've always been around; I just couldn't see them.

"So, Dean Wheeler committing suicide is a problem," I say. It isn't a question: their reaction made it clear.

"How's Rosa?" she says instead. "Seen much of her?"

I take a quick look at my smartphone. Eleven missed calls from her. It makes me feel... wanted? Making a mental note to call her back as soon as I can, I point at Maeve. "Don't change the subject. His suicide is bad. How?"

"Yes. Consider most people, when they die, have no idea about the reality they've been living in. Then they either ascend or stay in Hell in some form. Some, like you, get a second chance. But then, there're folks like me—aware of all this," Maeve says, spreading her arms wide, "before they pass. If a man like Dean Wheeler prepared for this, then he's dangerous. Look at the speed of his Strengthening. He's a cruel man who strives for domination. Being dead takes what he can do to a whole other level. Stalking unseen, persuasion of the spirit. Possession. God only knows what else. If he felt like he'd reached the limit of his power in life, his suicide may have been intentional."

Harry shuffles back in, holding a tray laden with cookies, a coffee pot and everything that goes with it. He sets it down with care in front of me. I think for a second as I pour out a little cream, enjoying the crackle and pop from the fire. The warmth is comforting.

"Harry," I begin, "it's a last resort, but the Amarok attack changes things. It's clear Wheeler knows his wife spoke to me and wants me out of the picture. He's planning something for her, and my only option left might be to Expunge him. Tonight."

Maeve shudders. Ghosts carry over tics like that from when they were human. It's like muscle memory, without the muscles.

Harry nods. "Two left. You must bring me more ingredients to craft more."

He moves to his bureau and unlocks a drawer with a

key kept on a chain around his neck. The Expungers—palm-sized, flat devices forged from iron and covered in infernal glyphs—are inside.

I can make them, but Harry likes to keep busy. Gathering the ingredients is the arduous part. Some are straightforward enough to gather, like garlic or holy water. The last items on the list are the dangerous ones—fae blood and wings. Now, these aren't Tinkerbelle-cute sprites with leaf dresses and dainty slippers. They're vicious, fanged sadists that delight in human suffering. I don't enjoy Expunging, but I'll gather the required items with pleasure if it means there are less fae in Hell.

I suppose I'll have to answer to Lilith herself one day. If Hell's taught me anything, it's that everything comes at a price.

Harry hands them to me. They're harmless to the living, but my fingers tingle when I touch them. Residue from my near-death experience.

"I'm thinking this isn't a straightforward haunting with intent to harm," I say, looking at Maeve, then Harry. "Let's track this. A proper piece of work delves into the— sorry, Maeve—occult, then commits suicide. What's the angle?"

"Power," Harry mutters with a shiver. I do, too. The air is frigid again, and I notice the flames in the fireplace are dying. "There's powerful magic in a meaningful sacrifice. Your demon friend Francis got it wrong, committing random murders; they didn't mean anything to him. The stronger the connection between the victim and the aggressor, the more potent the spell."

"And no one loved Dean Wheeler more than Dean fucking Wheeler."

"Precisely. He can never make it to heaven, but here, in Hell, he can use his own sacrifice to become more powerful than any ghost."

"Michelle Wheeler said her husband wanted to possess her. Maybe that's literal. He could control her every move that way, keep her a prisoner in her own body."

"And continue to run his empire like nothing had changed, with all the abilities of a Strengthened ghost."

"Sonofabitch..."

Maeve's been silent for a few moments. I glance at her, wondering what she's thinking, then realize she's frozen. It's like she's a video and someone's hit pause.

"Honey?" Harry says, standing in front of her and peering into her eyes. Her pupils move with frantic jerks. "Nick, can you..."

He doesn't finish. The fire snuffs out, plunging the study into darkness. Shooting to my feet, I grab an Expunger in one hand and my Ruger in the other. Green smoke slithers under the door, oozing into the room, writhing through the shadows. Dread clenches my stomach in its fist. I stagger against a table as my legs tremble. Harry's dropped to his knees, tears cascading down his cheeks.

A hooded figure stands by the study's door. Its presence steals the light, leaving just a black silhouette. My instincts scream at me like I'm in that alleyway again.

Wheeler.

For a second, Hell holds its breath.

Dean points at Harry. The old man lifts off the ground,

limbs stiff and splayed like Da Vinci's Vitruvian Man. I swing my revolver around, but his hooded head twitches in my direction and his eyes pin me in place. I can't move. I want to—Christ I *need* to—but my body just won't respond. Like having three bullet holes in my chest. Sweat beads on my forehead as I strain, but all I can do is watch.

Harry vibrates, teeth bared and clenched. Blood rushes from his eyes, nostrils and ears. Shit, his eyes! I can't look away as the crimson tears pour. He's begging with them, wide and disbelieving, pleading with Wheeler. Then he looks at Maeve and wails her name.

I want to scream too, but my jaw won't come loose. A mewling sound escapes through the gaps of my teeth. Instead, I weep as I watch my oldest friend's skin tear away from his body. Slices of it at first, but the curls of flesh come faster. He's like a pencil run through a sharpener. Blood gushes from widening tears, oozing to the floor in pools beneath his feet.

God, please, let it stop. Let me look away. *Please!*

My ears pop at the sudden intake of air, like Wheeler's sucking all the oxygen out of the room.

Harry implodes. One second he's there, suspended in mid-air, being flayed alive. The next, nothing but a crimson stain on the floor.

I blink as a spotlight shines down from above. My fear and grief wash away as its gentle warmth touches me. The Gates of Heaven are open, and they're calling Harry home. I've seen it a few times since my own ascension, though not everyone went up. More often than not, the opposite happened.

Someone else is watching the spectacle. Still unable to move, my eyes shift to the study's corner.

He's there. Charon. Gazing up at the light where the ceiling used to be. For a heartbeat, his eyes meet mine. I hear his voice reverberate in my mind.

Be seeing you, Holleran.

My eyes slide away from him. Charon's still there—I feel him—but it's like his business doesn't concern me anymore, and he doesn't want me staring. I look up into Heaven's light and see Harry's spirit. He smiles at me then looks at his wife and holds out his hand. Maeve's eyes continue to dart, her hand not moving to meet her husband's. And just like that, I understand.

Harry's ascending, and Wheeler's preventing Maeve from going with him.

I strain, fighting invisible restraints, but it's no good, Wheeler's holding me tight. My friends have waited for this moment for sixty years, and this dead asshole is denying them eternity together.

"*No!*"

Harry's voice echoes as he drifts upwards towards God's eternal embrace. He wants to stay if Maeve can't follow, but he's being forced upwards. It's out of his hands.

Wheeler's doing that too. People can reject ascension and stay if they want. But just like he's keeping me and Maeve frozen to the spot, he's pushing Harry through Heaven's Gates.

All I can do is watch as he becomes one with the light, and then it vanishes. The gates close.

Wheeler disappears too. The study's lights return, the

fireplace flickering back to life. I fall forward onto my face. I beat my Ruger's handle on the floor and scream my lungs dry.

He took my friend. My fucking friend. Worse, he split them up, and there's no changing that.

"Nick..."

Maeve's quiet whisper draws my attention. Her tears match mine, but she has a fortitude I can only wish for.

"I'm sorry," I spit out, kneeling in front of her. "I shoulda... I coulda..."

"It's not your fault," she says, looking up at the ceiling as if she hopes her husband can convince Heaven to open up again. Her voice wavers, on the verge of breaking.

I should never have come here. Wheeler wanted me—I knew that—and I came to them for help knowing it put them in the crosshairs. No one's safe around me until I deal with that bastard once and for all.

My eyes fall to a framed photo on the table. Climbing to my feet, I pick it up and stare at a black and white picture of Harry and Maeve when they were teenagers. Filled with love. Fucking hope for their future. It trembles in my grip.

I set it down, nod at Maeve without meeting her gaze, and head for the door.

"What will you do?" Maeve calls after me.

I turn.

"I'm gonna find Wheeler," I say, stuffing the Expungers in my pockets, "and make that sonofabitch pay. For everything."

REVENGE IS A DISH BEST SERVED...HOT

Haven feels deserted, like somehow the living, dead, and everything in between know to stay the fuck outta my way as I march towards Wheeler's place. I know he wants me, but I don't care why. I've got an Expunger with his fucking name on it.

The air has turned stagnant and the sticky heat becomes oppressive. My tie is loose and my collar button's open. The heat of the Expungers against my thigh overrides all else. It's like they're eager for action.

I share the sentiment as I race towards my destination; I'm just as eager to end the sonofabitch. Thoughts I've tried to suppress since he unloaded three bullets in my chest swirl in my mind—rage, anticipation. And shame. That most of all. This man killed me like I meant nothing, like I was an afterthought.

Now, my anger threatens to burn all that away. I can't shake the look in Harry's bulging eyes as his skin peeled from his face, as Wheeler tore him apart, and the way he reached out for Maeve when he realized he was losing her forever. The broken slump in Maeve's shoulders drives me on.

Revenge is a sin. It's one I plan to dirty my soul with.

Screw God, and fuck Hell too.

Vengeance is mine, says Nick Holleran.

The Wheeler estate sticks out like a gorilla in a monkey pen. Not for its size, though it is the kind of mansion the very worst asshole would own—three stories, a balcony on both sides, glass and white marble, and a swimmer's pool.

Right now, it's most noticeable feature is the swirling mass of green and purple cloud menacing the sky above. The dead must see if for miles around, and I wonder how the living *don't* notice. Then I realize that, on some level, they do. It's why they've emptied the streets.

There's no sound and the silence is unbearable. No car horns, no tires dragging, no music, no voices or footsteps. The absence of it all itches inside my skull. I wanna scream out loud, just to add some noise to the night.

Just to prove I can, but I fear that big, ol' swirling bruise might swallow any sound I make.

It's there, hovering above me, as I climb over the Wheeler's wall, staring down at me. Whatever's going on in that house is bad Juju. Real bad Juju.

I hum a song as I walk the perimeter of the building, a little habit I've had since I was a kid that calms my nerves when they're threatening to overwhelm, and I smile to myself when I realize the tune is *Bullet With Butterfly Wings* by The Smashing Pumpkins.

I tap the Expungers in my pocket. I've got a bullet for Wheeler.

With no signs of life, the mansion seems abandoned, but I know something inside is causing that fucked up sky. It's the only explanation. I ascend the steps to the double doors and reach out for the handle. They're not even locked. All too easy. Like I'm walking into a trap...

At least I *know* it's a trap, right?

There's one pressing matter left. I grab my smartphone and select Rosa's profile. Her image beams back at me, that photo I took in better times. Ignoring the list of missed calls, I send her a text instead.

Rosa, I'm sorry about tonight. I know I'm always letting you down. I'm sick and tired of it too. There's so much to explain. If you'll let me, I'd like to. Face to face. Nick.

As soon as I press send, I realize how stupid I've been. I might not make it out alive, and here I am trying to get Rosa to see me. Never really been an optimist, but there you go. Guess I am.

Or maybe I just couldn't spring the trap waiting for me without taking care of that unfinished business first. At least now she'll know I wanted it to work.

The same pregnant hush fills the Wheeler mansion. From my scouting of the exterior, I didn't see a single light in any of the rooms, not even the flicker of a candle, but *something's* causing that maelstrom. So that leaves the basement.

It narrows my search, at least. In my experience, houses this size take an age to investigate.

The clues are there, clear as day. Tendrils of green smoke, like the ones from Harry and Maeve's study, swirl around my ankles as I stride through the entry hall—an ethereal breadcrumb trail showing me the way.

It's too easy. My bones know it, but I don't give a fuck. My blood pumps fire, and my anger demands satisfaction.

The smoke leads me to a door behind the stairs; green

mist breathes from beneath. Glancing around, I almost shit myself as my eyeballs land on a larger-than-life portrait of none other than Dean Wheeler himself.

He's staring back at me, a smug smile on that cruel, cold face.

"I'm coming for you," I whisper, drinking in his features, the ones burned into my memory. "My face'll be the last one you ever see in Hell."

Pressing my ear to the door, I hear faint sobbing echoing from below. A woman. Michelle.

I'm done letting Dean fucking Wheeler hurt folk.

Well past done.

I go to draw my Ruger from its holster, then reconsider. It'll be as useful as a vomit-flavored lollipop against a ghost, consecrated bullets or not. Instead, I ease the door open and creep down the dark stairs. The energy swirling here makes the hair on my arms stand on end, makes my teeth itch. I flick my tongue over them; tastes like static. The green light throbs powerful, vibrant, as I descend, and I bare my teeth in a savage grin at the scene before me.

Michelle Wheeler lies on the floor, cowering and weeping, at the far side of a room lit by a hundred candles flickering with green flame. Mist boils across the floor. Standing before her, his washed-out back to me, is Dean Wheeler. Anger battles with excitement; I want to help Michelle, but the fact Dean hasn't seen me, doesn't know I've got the drop on him, almost makes my head spin with vengeful giddiness.

He's mine.

My attention's fixed on him, and I have no interest in

anything else. A filter of red hazes my vision as I stare at the scene, at Dean. The man who killed me. The piece of shit who tortured his wife, turned her into a living chew toy. The scumbag who hadn't gotten hard enough dominating her in life, and needed to do it in death too. The sonofabitch who flayed Harry alive and made the love of his life watch, helpless. Who forced him to Heaven alone, and trapped her here, in Hell, forever.

Revenge is a sin—I know this—but Dean Wheeler doesn't get to exist. Not anymore. Yanking an Expunger from my pocket, I charge towards him.

As I reach him and thrust my arm out, I see Michelle look up at me. I can't place the expression twisting the scars on her face. Relief? It must be.

The Expunger makes contact.

"Die, you fuck!" I scream, pushing against it with all my strength, as if I can ram it into the heart he doesn't have. The heart he *never* had.

Steam rises from it. Dean Wheeler lurches around to face me. I grin as I stare into his wide eyes. I want him to know that it's me that ended him, but Wheeler doesn't see me. The dead man stares into oblivion as realization dawns on him that the void is his eternal damnation.

His spirit unravels, like invisible hands have found the end of his thread and are pulling on it with all their might. From his head down to his toes, he disintegrates, steam hissing, his mouth open and slack in a soundless scream until it's no longer there.

And that's when my many mistakes hit home.

It wasn't relief. She was smiling.

Michelle Wheeler watches her husband's Expunging with delight painted across her ruined face. It hits me as Ruby's words from earlier slam into my head.

How'd she know Wheeler trailed her to your place? Could she see him?

She could see him. She's been able to see him all along.

Haste makes sloppy fucking work, Nick.

Only Wheeler's legs are visible, and they're deteriorating fast. His feet are standing inside a pentagram etched into the ground, and so are mine. Not just that. Stones with glyphs I don't recognize circle the pentagrams, petals from flowers and herbs crammed into the spaces in between.

Things I should have noticed, *would* have noticed on any other case. The name Dean Wheeler crawled into my head, made me lose my judgment, and it cost me.

Cost me big time.

I take a step forward, and it's like running into a window. Michelle had trapped Dean, and now she's done the same to me. We've both been pawns in her game. She's played it well, but she never had to.

She had me from the moment she told me her husband's name.

I set the trap off alright. I stepped right into the fucking thing, like a sap on a day trip to Disneyland.

Michelle circles her husband's pentagram, a knife in her hand. The runes etched into the steel flash as she brandishes it, ones that match the glyphs on the floor. The pain when she plunges it below my ribs drives me to my knees. I slide down the barrier keeping me trapped. My blood flows, pouring from my side and onto the ground, running in grooves cut into the stone floor. It trickles into my pentagram and fills it before spilling off into another groove, linking my trap with Dean's. Strength evaporates from my limbs. If the invisible wall didn't hold me up, I'd slump onto my face and die without a struggle.

Eyes are on me. I pull my stare from Dean's rapid disintegration, with just his feet left visible, and squint through the mist. Charon, that undead Clint Eastwood motherfucker, watches me. His words from earlier flood back into my mind.

Be seeing you.

I throw him a snarling grin. I ain't finished yet.

Michelle crouches before me, scarred cheeks flushed.

"When did you die?" I ask.

Most would ask 'why'd you do this?' but I figure she'll tell me anyway; the satisfied smile informs me she's the type to boast about her cleverness. I'm a captive audience until I bleed out. And what can I say? I'm a great listener.

"The first time? On our honeymoon. Dean choked me with a scarf he bought me from the hotel gift shop. I still have it in the closet. Never wore it after that though. See, it got him off. Never more aroused than when he was watching the light dying in my eyes. But I guess it was my fault. I introduced Dean to the occult in the first place. My mother told me stories when I was a little girl. She could *see*, Nick. Like you and me. She died in the asylum my father put her in. I never got to say goodbye before she passed. I wanted the chance, Mr. Holleran. I *longed* for it. I even told Dean. It piqued his interest, killing someone and bringing them back, dominating them in life and death. He took it to the next level, pushed my body to find my limit. I never did see my mother again. Maybe she just didn't miss me that much."

She spits on where Dean's remains would have fallen, but there's nothing there except my blood mixing with the artifacts. For a second, I feel a pang of pity for her, even though she's killed me. Murdered by both fucking Wheelers. I chuckle and blow a bubble of blood onto her.

Two things occur to me at once—her knife passed in through the barrier, and now my blood's passing out. Interesting.

"What's so funny, Mr. Holleran?"

"Please," I say, "call me Nick. No need to be formal now you've driven six inches of steel into me. How long have you planned this? Before or after you killed your husband."

"Oh, for quite some time, Nick. I've watched you with great interest since you began your second life." I glance at her bare feet and notice Michelle takes care not to step on either pentagram. She doesn't want to break the flow of blood. "You've earned your reputation for diligence, but there's nothing like the promise of revenge and a damsel in distress to make a man stupid. Especially when you add pressure and heat. I thought your bartender friend or maybe the ex-girlfriend would be the perfect motivation, but the old man and his wife were just too perfect."

"That was you?" I growl. "So you've been controlling him since his death?"

"Why not? This is my world. I introduced him to all of this, and you? You're just a fuck-up detective who wandered down the wrong alley. I *deserve* control." She laughs then. "I wonder how it burned him, being under my heel for a change. Oblivion must have been a relief to him."

"Michelle, you don't know enough if you think *anything* welcomes Expunging."

The mist billows and I see an altar at the rear of the basement room. Michelle walks to it in silence. I listen to her feet slap against the concrete. That's not all. The wind's howling outside, loud enough to make its presence known down here. The darkness swells and grows, dimming the candles, but that might just be my vision failing.

My blood continues to fill my pentagram, the excess flooding into Dean's. Michelle approaches, holding an Expunger. I can only shake my head. She's played me for a sucker.

"The erasing of a spirit as evil as my husband's, by a man he murdered, is a powerful sacrifice. Death links your souls. You know what would be even stronger?"

"Enlighten me," I reply, though I can read between the lines.

"The sacrifice of a soul that's lived twice, tainted by revenge." Michelle crouches, those beautiful, bronze eyes staring into mine. "People have dominated me my whole life, Nick. My father had...appetites, and with my mother out of the picture, they only grew. And then there was Dean. The perfect husband, on the surface, but behind closed doors... I used to think he could keep me safe from men like my father. Turned out it was just more of the same. I don't need them anymore. It's my turn to be in control. For eternity."

She reaches out to me, as if to caress my face, but stops herself.

"You're the key. Thank you for your sacrifice."

Listen, I'm half-dead for the second time, face pressed up against a wall of magic and blood dripping off my chin. Charon's staring at me like a lion watching a gazelle, and the wind outside's howling so loud I figure the windows upstairs have shattered. But I'm not going down without a fight. I've got a plan.

No idea if it'll work, but I'm out of options and any plan's better than none.

"Sorry, lady. Your life sounds like Hell, literally, but you're not getting away with what you've done tonight. And it looks I'm going downstairs anyway, so..."

Smiling my boyish, lopsided grin, I pull my Ruger from its holster.

Michelle Wheeler's eyes widen as I aim at her and pull the trigger. The bang echoes through the small room. Her brains splatter the altar and her body topples to the ground. Her leg sprawls across the grooves on the floor, sending the glyph stones flying, breaking the circle.

I fall forward, released from the pentagram, and crash face-first into the stone floor, arms too weak to catch my fall.

"My luck's in," I say out loud, for reasons that escape me.

I struggle to my knees. Charon's waiting, and I don't wanna die on my face. A cold numbness is setting in, telling me I haven't got long left.

The wind howls inside the basement as, like clock-work, Michelle's spirit rises from her dead body. No warm glow beckons her. Heaven's Gates are shut.

Revenge is a sin, and even though Dean deserved it, killing him and making it look like a suicide is still murder.

Not to mention the business she conducted tonight.

The basement's cold, like the grave. Charon flows forward, a shadow rippling across the wall, and halts beside Michelle. He bends to whisper in her ear. Fear floods her face at his words; words she won't have time to forget like I did.

I fish my last Expunger from my pocket and toss it at her, then I look away, screw my eyes shut. Despite what she's done, I've no desire to see it carry out its work.

I count to twenty before I open my eyes. The wind's bluster has stopped, and the green flames have died, plunging the basement into darkness. I crane my neck to stare at the ceiling, hoping against hope that they view my deeds tonight as just, or else forgive me for services rendered. Will the Gates of Heaven open for me again? Miracles happen, right?

A second passes.

Then another.

A third.

"You're looking in the wrong direction, you know."

The voice is silk. It's like every accent I've ever heard rolled into one. It's at once intoxicating and terrifying. I can't hold my head up any longer and it drops. I can't move from my knees.

A figure steps from behind me and crouches to peer into my face. At first, I think he's a Nephilim. His intimidating size, his vibrant color, his sharp features remind me of Suraz, but his sheer presence tells me he's something more, and he doesn't wear armor. Instead, he's draped in a crimson robe. His stare is like a weight smothering my mind. His golden eyes hold the knowledge of eternity and, unlike Suraz, he's bearded, black hair styled to perfection.

Nephilim are beautiful. This being is beyond that.

Shit. He's an Angel. A fallen *Angel.*

"Lucifer?" I cough, blood dribbling down my chin.

Satan smiles and produces the whitest piece of cloth I've ever seen. It's a shame when he presses it against my mouth and cleans away the blood dripping from my lips.

"I should thank you," he says, glancing down at the pentagrams and artifacts. "I suspect I would not have enjoyed what Michelle Wheeler had in store for me."

He's urbane. Jovial, almost. Fucking Lucifer seems like a nice guy. Who knew?

"What do you mean?" I ask, and sway forwards. The Devil himself holds me upright with the little finger of his left hand.

"The woman had clearly done her research. These sacrifices aren't something I could just ignore. You have my brother to thank for that." He points to the ceiling. "He does so love his obscure rules and laws. Unless they concern him, of course. But then, maybe there's a reason hypocrisy isn't on his list of sins. Oh well. Anyway, a spell this powerful is not a mere invocation. It's a binding. I would have had to carry out Michelle's every command. Anything within my power would be hers. My agents have worked hard to conceal that knowledge, and how she found it puzzles me. I suppose that's a question for another time."

"Right..."

I'm so fucking tired. Wait... Brother?

"Your brain is not working as it should, my friend. Understandable."

Lucifer taps me on the cheek with a light touch. It feels like the time Rosa slapped me. The fog clouding my brain thins for a second.

Did he just say God's his damned brother?

"Excellent news. You completed the ceremony when you Expunged Michelle. Lucky for you, healing is a skill I excel in, so why not command me to mend your broken body, and we shall part as friends?"

He blows into his palms and rubs them together, like he's firing up the magic.

"Wait!" I shout, a reserve of strength coming from somewhere.

He fixes me with those million-dollar eyes, like he's reminding me to be very careful with my next words. But the Devil is at my beck and call. I want to make this good.

"There's a soul trapped here. A good one. She meant to ascend decades ago but didn't. Her name's Maeve Wells. Can you do it? Send her to Heaven to be with her husband? He departed today. Michelle, she..."

A hacking cough interrupts me, sending warm blood down my chin. I'm hoping he got the point.

Lucifer rises to his feet and glances around the room, shock etched into his obsidian features. He stares at Michelle's corpse, then back at me. He crouches again. The Devil produces his white cloth, somehow unstained, and dabs at my face.

"Human, that is the first time I have felt something other than apathy in millennia. Eternal life is quite boring, you know? You would sacrifice your life for the chance to reunite a couple in Heaven? You *do* realize those pearly gates don't wait for you? When your body gives up in one hundred and ninety-four seconds, you are staying in Hell. In His book, revenge is revenge."

I nod. There isn't a second thought in my mind.

"Done," Lucifer says, with a thunderous clap.

He stands and looks up at the ceiling. I can see in his eyes that he sees straight through it; his gaze goes directly to the Heaven.

Smiling, he glances down at me, the grin turning to a frown. I flinch as our eyes meet. Somehow, I know I shouldn't be able to withstand his sheer presence. Maybe it's because I'm almost dead, or maybe it's the effect of the sacrifice.

"You know what? I am in a fine mood, Nick Holleran. You have surprised me, and that occurs all too seldom in Hell. This will not do at all. This is my kingdom. I have fulfilled the terms of our contract, and I am not meant to meddle in the lives of humans. His Rules." The Devil grins at me. "Fuck them."

Lucifer crouches and lays his palm against my side. It's like lightning's struck me. He holds me down with his other hand as I gasp and convulse, as power blasts through my body, blowing away the cobwebs in my mind, healing the cracks in my bones and the tears in my flesh. It hurts—Christ, it hurts so goddamn much—but I feel alive. More than I ever have before. He lets go and I spring to my feet, ready to run the New York Marathon.

"Fixed that rib too," he says, with a wink. "Now, if that is all? You need to stay out of trouble, Holleran. Only one life left."

"Wait," I shout, as he moves by me, patting myself down. Blood soaks my shirt but, underneath, my skin's unblemished and I feel like I've slept for a month. "I need to know something. Why is the world like this? Why are we all in Hell? I thought God was your father?"

Lucifer pauses, his back to me. He looks over his shoulder, golden eyes narrowed.

"Father. Yes, that is how they like to tell it," he says, turning to face me. The sheer force of his will batters against me as his stare penetrates mine. "I suppose there is no harm. The one you call God is my brother. He cast me and my supporters out of Heaven, thousands of years ago. They got that part correct. Back then, there wasn't a Hell. God created it for those who supported me. Humans included." He places a hand on my shoulder. It's like being squashed by a bus. "Your people were always the most loyal to me. Now you have to prove yourselves before you are allowed back home, and my brother is rather fickle."

With that last word, Lucifer spins and strides into the darkness at the end of the basement. The candles spurt back into life, orange flames illuminating the room. I gaze at Michelle's corpse, then holster my Ruger.

"One life left, Nick," I murmur, turning my back and heading for the stairs, lost in my thoughts as I ponder the Devil's revelations.

EPILOGUE

AFTER ... SEPTEMBER 21st

"Next Friday then?" I say, pausing for Rosa's reply.

I flick my eyes to the girl in the corner. I wonder if Darcy can hear the excitement in my voice, or if she listens at all.

"Okay," Rosa replies, "it's a date then. Wear something nice, and no ghost stories, okay? I don't care how many dead guys are in the restaurant with us."

"Have it your way." I laugh. "Deal."

"See you Friday, Nick Holleran."

"See you then. And Rosa?"

A pause.

"Yeah?"

"Thank you."

"Don't thank me yet, big guy. You suck at first dates."

She laughs as she hangs up. I whoop as I lean back in my chair and reach for my packet of cigarettes. I pull one out and go to light it, staring at the beautiful day outside my window.

"They'll kill you, you know?"

The cigarette hangs from my lip as I turn, dumbfounded, towards Darcy. That girl has haunted my office in silence for at least five years. Now, she's standing on the other side of my desk, so close I can feel the flames licking from her empty eye sockets.

My cigarette falls to the floor.

"Can I help you?" I ask.

It's all I can think of to say. Better than nothing.

"Yes, Mr. Holleran," she says. "I have a case for you. I want you to find out who murdered me."

THE END

THE DEVIL WALKS IN BLOOD
BOOK TWO

PROLOGUE

CHILD OF NATURE

From the sidewalk, I watch Nick Holleran through his office window. The man should have died. Again. Mystery swirls in Hell. Questions with elusive answers that I must uncover.

A wind threatens to stir, but dies, just like that. The air is heavy—so thick I can taste the coming rain on my tongue. He arrives. Lucifer. The Master of Hell, and someone I have served for eons. He views me as a friend, perhaps more, but how can one such as he have companions?

He exists to lead; I am made to follow.

His hand clamps on my shoulder. The weight makes my knees buckle. That is the Devil for you. He does not try to dominate; he just *does*.

Despite that, he wishes for peace and solitude. His selflessness strikes me. Always has. Even when he led his armies against God, he did it for the humans, for those of us in Heaven who chafed against God's rule. Since the Great Divide, I can count on one hand the number of times he's intervened with events in Hell. It has not happened since the Dark Ages.

And then, last night...

His fingers rest on my shoulder still, and though I should be well used to his presence now, I can hide nothing from him. The question forces its way from the tip of my tongue and onto my lips.

"Why did you spare the human? Holleran's stuck in Hell, even after death. He knows that. There is no ticket into Heaven for him. Revenge is a sin, and in the eyes of God, he is guilty."

Sometimes, no matter how I struggle, no matter the years together, the battles we fought and the quiet times of reflection, I just don't *get* Lucifer.

This is one of those occasions. You'd think some clarity would reach me, that I could understand even one thing he does. Perhaps I overestimate my worth—it's not for me, Suraz, mightiest of Lucifer's Nephilim, to understand him.

Still, now and then, Lucifer forces me to question him, to wonder if I picked the correct side, all those years ago.

No, Suraz, you have made your peace with that. You chose the path to walk, there is no returning.

"Sparing the human... I might ask you the same thing, Suraz." His voice is a murmur, but it rolls like approaching thunder. The rich baritone still makes me shudder. His voice threatens to overwhelm my senses, and I wonder how a mere human like Holleran coped in Lucifer's presence. "Didn't you save him from a demon, out for revenge? Perhaps you inspired me. You certainly made enough of a mess. Ruby's still cleaning the demon ichor off the floor, poor woman."

"You were watching?"

"Always. I wondered what you saw in that place. The Styx. Is it her? The owner? Do you think I should get to know her better?"

Lucifer is in a rare mood. He's jovial. Playful almost.

I glance from the corner of my eye, tilting my head upwards at his face, and see him smiling as we hug the lengthening shadows of the late afternoon day, watching Holleran together. We ignore the Haven City drizzle as it drifts onto grey streets. I don't know what drew me here, what compelled me to watch through the detective's window. It concerns me that Lucifer felt the same pull.

I let my gaze linger as I struggle to recall the last time I stood in Lucifer's presence. Time's a funny thing when you've lived for an eternity. The concept slips in my mind. It could have been months or decades, and my...vices don't help my memory.

Spirits drift amongst the ignorant humans scurrying about Haven, blind to what surrounds them. Elsewhere, monsters and demons and malevolent forces lurk. Despite it all, the late-afternoon holds a strange quality. Even the Devil's presence doesn't account for it.

I frown, considering Lucifer's words. "The demon would have killed Holleran. He may have meddled in affairs beyond his comprehension, but he acted with honor. I saw justice dispensed."

"If Holleran didn't 'meddle', who would? *You*? The Nephilim? Absin is absent all too often, and you're spending much time at The Styx these days, my old friend. Are you taking up another vice or sharpening an old one?"

Anger makes my head spin. With a snarl, I face Lucifer. A head taller than me, my 'old friend' could crush me with a thought. Right now, all I can think of are the decisions the Devil made that led me here. Banished from Heaven, unable to die or return home. They plague me. Always. Millennia of doubt and regret because of loyalty to my master. My friend.

His golden eyes, framed by his obsidian skin, narrow, but one side of his mouth curves upwards. The smug bastard.

"Hell's pulse beats beneath The Styx," I snap, defensive. "Information flows there and someone must control the current. As for Absin, she feels the Seal's pull, as you well know. She lingers there, as if the rest of Hell has ceased to exist. Besides, if this human is so precious to you, you're lucky I spent the evening drinking."

The smile turns into a full grin as Lucifer holds up a hand.

"Peace, Suraz. I understand." Sudden sadness flits across his features. "You've experienced perfection. Lived it and had it ripped from you. It's natural you seek to fill that hole, however you can."

Lucifer drops his gaze to my forearms, as though he can see the track marks under my clothes. Of *course* he would know. Pity washes over his face before turning back to Holleran's office. My anger, always writhing in the murky waters of my corrupt soul, sinks beneath the surface once more.

There are some things I still can keep from the Devil— secrets that are mine to carry—though I punish myself for them. One day, he'll uncover them.

I blame Lucifer for my failings. When we warred

against God, he didn't coerce me. I rose to the challenge, and led our armies, humans included, into the fray. Memories of Lucifer, prostrating himself before his brother, flood my mind. Gritting my teeth, I force them away.

"What brings you from the lower levels?" I ask instead. It isn't often Lucifer spends time on Hell's surface.

"Rituals and occult magic. What else?" Lucifer sighs, and Hell groans at the sound. "Michelle Wheeler had everything she needed. A dual sacrifice. A cardinal sin. She even fooled our detective into helping her. She pressed his buttons so well I almost admired her for it." He points towards Holleran's back, framed by the light flooding through his window. The human talks on his cell phone, oblivious to the Devil's sympathy. "We were very lucky. If she'd chosen anyone else, she might not have been stopped, and I'd be obliged to provide a very dangerous woman with some exclusive privileges in our little corner of Hell. You can blame my brother and his fucking rules for that."

I grunt, a noise that could almost pass for a laugh. "With Holleran breathing, I take it you broke a few of those."

Lucifer shrugs. "Let's say I misinterpreted them. Hell is mine, and so are the humans that don't reach God's," and his mouth twists when he says, "lofty standards. If my brother has a problem with me sparing Holleran and sending another soul through His gates, He knows how to reach me."

"What brings you here? Does the human compel you so much?"

Lucifer keeps his counsel. His concentration is like a physical presence. I follow his stare and see the human jump with shock as he turns to his window. The cigarette he smokes sticks to his lip. Beside me, Lucifer cocks his head and smiles.

"Hell stirs," he says, turning that penetrating gaze on me. I feel tiny in his presence. Meaningless in the face of such magnificence. "The layers merge, and beings that shouldn't escape the lower levels bubble to the surface. *Two* Amarok stalked Holleran last night. They say there are Wendigo in the forest. The Wheeler woman uncovered ways to summon me and bind me to her will; how? Even now, I feel the disease of an Amhuluk, and they've kept to the lower levels for centuries. Those Dagon cults in New England stir again. And that's just America. All across Hell, humans are discovering the nature of their existence faster than before. Some are seeking the unseen creatures, demons and deceased, for good or ill. Curiosity is in their nature, but I feel destiny is forcing the issue. Your friend Absin's instinct is correct; the Seal weakens, well before its time. A showdown approaches—I don't know when or how—but it's between my brother and I. This time, I won't surrender. We deserve more than this. All of us."

For millennia, Lucifer has offered little more than sardonic wit and disinterest. Passion lights a fire in his soul once more. I often put his disinterest down to melancholy. He never encouraged the humans to follow him in his war against God, but he fought, and lost, for them.

"A war with Heaven?" I whisper, trepidation battling with eagerness.

Lucifer shakes his head. "It may come to that. All I know is this: the weather's changing. I can smell it in the air.

And, in the eye of this gathering storm, stands Nick Holleran. The human has plagued my resting mind of late, and our meeting confirmed his importance. Watch him, Suraz. For me. Guide him, if you can."

Lucifer caresses my face; his touch thrills my skin. I close my eyes to savor it. The sensation reminds me of Heaven. My master. My friend. More than that. Oh, how I wish for more.

But he will never give it.

"Suraz," Lucifer whispers. He's looking into my eyes, my very essence. The Devil smiles. "Holleran has one life left. See he doesn't waste it. Every human dies, but I feel as though his passing must achieve some purpose first."

Lucifer dissolves into the waiting shadows, and his sudden absence hits me like a body blow. Shaking my head, clearing the fog from my mind, I gaze across the street, up at the human's office.

"Nick Holleran," I whisper, tracing where Lucifer's fingers grazed my skin. "What makes you so important?"

I, ME, MINE

SEPTEMBER 21st
HAVEN CITY, OREGON

"A case?" I mutter.

My cigarette flutters from my lips to the floor, smoke tendrils drifting upwards. I can't see myself, and I'm glad the eyeless ghost-girl who's stood in the corner of my office for the last five years can't either. At least, I think she can't. Reckon I must look as surprised as a fish that got the hook in the wrong end.

"A fucking case? You haven't so much as twitched for five years, and now you're offering me a job. How're you even gonna pay?"

It isn't my best quip, but under the circumstances...

She cocks her head, twisting around until she's facing my laptop.

"Can you turn that racket off?"

I blink. Nirvana's *Stay Away* plays, on a low volume I might add, and my fingers feel thick as I hit pause. "What, you don't like my music?"

"Is that what you call it? I prefer a little more...melody

in mine. Don't you have any Beatles records?"

"Records?" I ask, glancing at Spotify. "Wait, what the Hell are we talking about? I don't even know your real name!"

"It's Diana."

Not Darcy, the name I gave her. I'm actually kind of disappointed.

"Close enough, I guess. Okay, so why's it taken you five years to speak to me? I've tried, you know. More than once."

She turns her sockets on me and my blood chills a few degrees. It's like those eyeless pits pin me to the chair. They see everything; I'm sure of that.

The analytical part of my brain fights its way to the surface as I study her. With her eyes missing and her black skin now grey, washed out like all ghosts, it's hard to place an age on her, but I'd guess no more than sixteen. Max. Her long, pigtailed hair runs down to her waist, and she's wearing a striped, one-piece dress that stops just above her knees. Not from this decade. The 1960s, if that comment about 'Beatles records' is any indicator. I lean back in my chair, waiting for her to answer.

Girl could've stood in that corner for sixty years, if I'm right. A life sentence for a victim.

She shrugs, just a bump from those slim shoulders. "I don't know... Part of me noticed you, but it's like a haze. Your name, what you do, the people who visit you." Her mouth curves into the hint of a smile. "The conversations you have with Rosa. Your music. It washes over me, but some of it sticks. Most of the time all I can think about is his face. The man who killed me, leering at me as I fight for air. As he takes my eyes. The memory smothers me, but for a while now, I saw more. Heard more, like... I knew when you were here, and when you left. Who visited you. Just now, it lifted. I can't explain it."

"Yeah, it's been a strange couple days," I whisper, rubbing my eyes.

That's the understatement of the year. My last case—shit, was it really only yesterday?—dragged me right back to the night I died. The night when all this started.

His name was Dean Wheeler, a crook with enough enemies to hire a P.I. to follow him, and with enough paranoia to lure a tail into a dark alley. That's how I wound up with three bullets in my chest and the power to see the dead.

Then his wife arrives in my office, mutilated and fearful, telling me she's being followed by Dean. The *ghost* of Dean. Needless to say, I went flying into the fray. The next thing I know, one of my best friends gets murdered in front of me, and I'm breaking into Wheeler's villa, out for blood. Only I'm the one who winds up bleeding, a sacrifice in Michelle Wheeler's ritual to summon Lucifer and wreak her revenge on the world.

Can't say I blamed her, but I'll be damned—literally—if I'm going to be anyone's sacrifice. See, her sigils could hold me, but they couldn't hold a bullet. Two Wheelers turned out to be exactly the kind of offering that'd attract the Devil and so I wound up with the most powerful being in Hell on the hook.

I surprised him when I didn't beg for my own life. I asked him to reunite two souls in Heaven. Guess maybe I made an impression. I could have asked for anything, so I figure he saved me for services rendered, but those scales feel unbalanced. Pretty sure I'll be seeing him around.

Diana's watching me—at least, I think she is—and I realize I've been sitting in silence a little too long. It's been a fucking long couple of days.

I fill a glass with bourbon, and almost ask if she wants one. I'm not sure if it's her age, or the fact she's a goddamn ghost that stops me in my tracks. "You died in this room."

She nods, recognizing the statement in my tone. I don't need to ask. Ghosts who haven't Strengthened live out spiritual loops of their lives, usually their last moments. Why else would she be here, of all places?

"He brought me here when he..."

Her head sinks. I regret bringing it up, but...

I'm taking her case. I already know it.

I down the bourbon, then climb to my feet. She's just a kid—murdered in my office—and I don't want to question her here. I ain't visited the alley I died in yet, and I'm not sure I want to. Dream about it often enough.

"Want some fresh air? Sorry, figure of speech. Let's go outside. Change of scenery might do you some good."

I grab my spare trench coat—not my favorite, but I set that one alight yesterday trying to scare off two fucking Amaroks—and walk to the door. Her reflection wavers in the glass, hesitating.

She follows me with slow, tentative steps when I swing the door open. I guess it's been a while since she stepped outside.

...

"You know, Kurt Cobain loved The Beatles."

"Who's Kurt Cobain?" Diana asks, walking by my side.

I sigh. So, my small talk's weak right now. I'm a little shook. After the events at the Wheeler place last night, I should've gone home, taken it easy and let what happened sink in. Hell, I should have gone to bed for a night or two at least.

Maeve and Harry moved on yesterday—to Heaven, but I lost `em just the same. It comforts me they're together, and I owe Lucifer for that. Michelle Wheeler would have stranded Maeve in Hell if she'd had her way.

Not that I knew it was her. She pinned it on Dean, used my rage and vengeance to feed her ritual. Man, did my soul sing when I Expunged that sonofabitch, but I sealed my fate in the process. Even if the Devil took pity and saved me from the Reaper's swing, revenge is a sin. Reckon no matter what I do, Heaven's closed to me now.

Not like I'm giving up. Too stubborn or plain stupid. My old ma always said I fought for everything, bless her soul, and yeah, that phrase contains a healthy dollop of sarcasm. Since my awakening, I've avoided visiting my family home. I don't want to know what I'll find now that I can see the dead and the demons.

Haven't been there in years, even before my death. I moved to Haven from Portland a lifetime ago and never looked back, even if my thoughts sometimes stray that way.

I put my restlessness down to Lucifer's healing. I made my way back to my office after our encounter, but I can't recall the details. Think I just sat in my chair for a spell, then got back to work. Still, I bled out on the floor of Michelle Wheeler's basement, just like I did in that alleyway. The Devil might have healed me, made me feel fitter than I have in years, but the crash is going to be like all my hangovers rolled into one.

Damn, I haven't slept in over forty-eight hours.

Maybe that's why I can't nail my thoughts down. My mind's ragged from a night of raw revelation, but right now all I want is something to focus on. A new case. Someone to help.

Diana glides by my side, head tracking like a security camera, taking in every part of this strange, new world she's seeing for the first time. I wonder what it all looks like when you have no eyes.

"Where are we going?" she asks, voice shrill, like she's standing on the edge of panic.

Shit.

I ain't thinking straight. This kid hasn't seen a lick of Haven, save for my office wall, in sixty years. Place has changed—so have the people—and I don't just mean the dead. Folk of all colors and shapes, dressed in clothes I reckon boggle her poor mind, are streaming by, way more than she'd have seen back in the 60s. Vehicles fill the road too, blaring horns, spitting fumes, pounding bass.

This is like my awakening squared. It's not just ghosts for her. It's *everything*. She's been transported sixty years into the future.

"To my apartment. It ain't far. Sorry, guess I'm not thinking straight today. Can you blame me?"

I offer her my lopsided smile. The boyish, charming

one. She peers up at me, jaw like stone. Now that I think about it, this grin don't work out all too well for me.

"Is it close?"

I throw a glance around. My feet walked me here on autopilot while I did some first class navel-gazing.

"Yeah, yeah. It's not even a minute's walk from here. Come on."

Picking up the pace, Diana follows, so close I can feel the chill in the seam where we're occupying the same space. She's got her head down, avoiding the sensory assault, so I scan the street for the two of us. That's when I see it.

An unmarked cop car sits across from my apartment. How do I know it's the cops? Because these pains in the ass tail me and shake me down whenever they get the chance. Or they're bored. Maybe it's for kicks? I never did ask.

Lori Gavin and Henry Butler. Yeah, I have history with these two morons. Our professional disagreements go all the way back to when I worked regular P.I. jobs. I understood their beef better back then. Not all cops like freelancers, especially not ones who took cases for shady people on the side.

Look, money talks, alright? I learned my goddamn lesson when three bullets pinned me to the ground in a filthy alleyway.

Except that now, they like me even less. They damn-near accuse me of planting evidence and taking advantage of the sickos—their words—with my paranormal shtick.

My paranormal shtick landed me face-to-face with the Devil last night and now a ghost just followed me back from my office. I'm not in the mood for their shit right now.

Fuck, what if they know about last night? They couldn't, right? Cops would have come by the office with a warrant.

It's a shakedown, that's all. A good, ol' Haven PD violation of civil rights.

Still...

"Change of plans, kid. Know somewhere better we can go. It'll help you settle in more." I lower my voice. "I hope..."

Turning on my heel, I stoop, half-jogging in some weird, goblin-like lurch, and head back the way we came, Diana still stuck to my side. No questions... Gotta say, not my style, but I appreciate it.

We pass my office and I take a peek. I always do when I ramble by. I double-take.

"Did you see something up there?"

"Where?" Diana squeaks, head down.

"My office. Thought I saw..."

I don't say 'a shadow'. It's the lack of sleep, the last couple of days catching up to me, the goddamn cops outside my apartment. Even one of those would be enough to put a guy on edge.

"What?"

I skid to a stop and peer into the darkness across the sidewalk. Sun's setting real quick in Haven these days.

"Nothing."

I'm lying. It ain't the window now. A glance confirms I saw nothing. But there are eyes watching me. Not the crushing weight of Lucifer's gaze like at the Wheelers' place, but similar. My mouth goes dry and my bones start to ache. That presence is like a shadow at the corner of my eye, like an itch in my spine.

Maybe it's my imagination. Again. The bastard.

"Thought I saw something..."

"I don't see a thing," the girl answers.

Her eyeless stare dawns on me. Show's how fucking frazzled I am. Hey, ghost-girl with no eyes, did you see something? Get a grip, Nick. "That a joke? Just I'm not sure if I should laugh or not."

Her expression doesn't change, but I feel like Diana just rolled her eyes.

"I can see, you idiot. Not how I did before I died, but it'll do. Just all this out here... It's a lot to take in."

"Right," I say, glancing around.

That pressure from somewhere ebbs away, and my breath comes that little bit easier again. Maybe I'm on the verge of a panic attack?

Saturday evening travellers jam the rain-slick, neon-lit sidewalk. It's not just the living, finishing work and heading out for the night; the dead walk beside them. Hell thrives, and the city's buzz threatens to explode.

Some ghosts do journey here and there, aware and living a different kind of existence. Some nod at me as they pass by, recognizing me as aware. Others just stand around, lost in the cycle of their afterlife. Walking once more, I cross the kneeling, bearded man. He still weeps as he holds out his hands, like he's done for the past five years and God knows how much longer.

"He blames himself for the death of his son."

I freeze and look back. Diana's stopped in front of the other ghost, staring at him.

"They argued on the sidewalk, and his boy turned

and ran. As he did, he slipped, and cracked his head on the ground. An accident, but he blames himself, and all that's left inside is grief. He took his own life and returned here in death."

"You knew him?" I ask, pulling a cigarette from my pocket and sheltering it while I light it. I'm hoping it'll settle my nerves.

"No," Diana says, turning away, "but I feel his pain. And those will kill you, you know? Daddy always hated smoking."

A ghost runs ahead of us, a gun in hand. He pauses, lifts the weapon to his head and blows his brains out in an act of silent suicide. He drops to the sidewalk, flickers, then disappears.

Fella's caught in a loop. He kills himself every twenty minutes.

His performance doesn't faze me now, and all the oblivious, living faces passing it by almost bring a smile to my face. Life is a farce sometimes.

The first time I saw it, I drew my weapon in self-defense. Man, I'm lucky no one saw that.

I ponder Diana's words for another couple of seconds. A ghost feeling the 'pain' of another isn't something I've come across. My first thought is to take her to Harry and Maeve's, but after last night, that's not an option for obvious reasons. I swallow the pang of sadness, hiding it deep in my stomach. I'll deal with that another time.

Still, there's another place we can talk in safety, and that's my Plan B: The Styx. That's if Ruby ain't still pissed at me. It's not like *I* killed the demon in her bar last night.

"Come on," I say, checking both ways before crossing the street. Like Lucifer said at the Wheelers' place, I've only got one life left. I'd rather not waste it on something dumb like getting hit by a car. "We're not far."

I could have driven, I guess. I run a classic, bottle-green 1994 Ford Mustang convertible. She's a beauty, no doubt, but I know a shortcut to The Styx through Meadow Park. A lungful of fresh air will do me some good, if not my new client.

Plus, if the cops *are* looking for me, they'll know my ride. It stands out.

The park isn't a place I'd recommend many to walk through after dark, despite the pretty name, but I can look after myself. For the most part.

A thin mist smothers the grass. It ain't that cold, and it's raining. Night turned dark fast too. Quicker than it should, I'm pretty sure. Weird things happen in Hell every Godforsaken day, but the fucking hairs on the back of my neck are on end and my gums are starting to throb. I pull the collar up on my trench coat, trying to keep warm as my muscles bunch up.

Call me Detective Fucking Obvious, but something ain't right.

"You gonna ask me questions, Nick?" Diana whispers.

I glance at her again and curse as I look into the holes where her eyes used to be. They freak me out. I'm not squeamish, but her killer must've done that to her before she died, and that's what bothers me. Some humans are thralls or influenced by malevolent demons—something I discovered in great detail during the Whiskey Pete's case almost four years ago—but just as many have evil festering in their souls. To do something like that to her, they had to have been cracked one way or the other.

Still, I need to get a lid on my reactions, for her sake.

I'll reserve judgment on Diana's killer until I learn more. *If* I learn more. I'm expecting her murderer's already dead. Then what?

"When we get to where we're going," I say, pointing across the foggy park. "I like to ask my questions while sitting down. Usually in my office, but needs must."

"Hmm, you're lying. I can tell. Talking of your office and telling lies, I couldn't help overhearing before, your talk with Rosa? You're really terrible with women."

I laugh, and it feels good. The sound rings out like it's trying to dispel the gloom. Now my teeth ache right along with my gums.

"You know, dating's changed a lot since 1960. Were you even old enough to date anyway?"

"I died in 1968. And, yeah, I'm old enough. I'm fifteen. Didn't have a lot of time for it though. Had to help my momma raise four babies, worked split shifts at the diner and the Laundromat. Only way to keep a roof over our heads."

My laughter dies. Black kids have it tough nowadays. Can't imagine Haven during the 60s. I think about Diana's family after she died. She didn't mention her dad then. Had he passed before she did? Did they ever discover what happened to her?

The answer, though it happened decades ago, pisses me off.

No. They didn't.

The local PD wouldn't have wasted resources looking into a missing girl from a poor, black family.

"Don't get me wrong. I'm not a proud man. I'll take all the help I can get." I'm hoping falling on my sword might help to change the subject. "What am I doing wrong? With Rosa, I mean?"

"What are you waiting for? You're always putting things off with her. Now you've arranged another date for six days away. Something's going to come up. Isn't that what you always say? 'Something's come up.' See her tomorrow. You're lucky she's hanging around for you at all."

That's what I get for letting my guard down, I guess. A fifteen-year-old girl who died fifty-six years ago just let me have it with both barrels.

"Well," I say, floundering. "It's not that easy. The last few years hit me pretty hard, you know? Intense ain't the word, kid, and yesterday's shit show needs a few days to settle. Now there's *this*."

"See? 'Something's come up, Rosa.' I ain't going anywhere, Nick. Don't use me as an excuse."

I scowl in response and shove my hands deep into my pockets. I reckon my bottom lip's sticking out too. We walk in silence, wet grass squelching beneath my feet. I can feel the cold mist seeping through my pant legs, city lights fading as we weave deeper into the park. Diana doesn't make a sound.

Nothing makes a sound.

The mist's getting thicker. It's not natural. My stomach sinks. I pat the Ruger-57 under my arm. It can harm humans and some lesser demons, but there's more than that out there.

I don't even have a sliver of iron.

"Diana," I hiss, pausing and drawing my gun. "Stick close to me."

I'd like to say she'll be safe, since she's a ghost, but there's entities that'll make a ghost deader than their first time in Hell.

My breathing's loud in my ears as I peer through the fog. The temperature plummets, and I wish I'd never stepped foot in goddamn Meadow Park. My fingers grip the Ruger's alloy steel and I bare my teeth in a silent snarl.

The stench of rot grows thick in my nostrils and in the distance I hear a ragged breath, like a body dragged through gravel.

"You haven't escaped the call, Nick Holleran." It's a voice I recognize, one that sounds like fingernails clawing at sandpaper. "I am here to collect."

I curse. Louder than I should with a kid present.

I turn, spreading my hands out wide, the Ruger hanging loose. It'd have no effect on Charon anyway.

"Ferryman, long time no see."

I give him my best grin. It doesn't affect him. Nothing does. He sees Hell in black and white. You're alive or dead, and if you ain't breathing, you're Charon's business.

Yeah, we've crossed paths before. But never like this.

"You should have died, Nick Holleran. Again. That you live vexes me. Let us see to that."

YOU CAN'T DO THAT

"Last time I checked—and believe me, Charon, I've done that more than once since last night—I'm breathing. You've no business with me, pal."

The ferryman just stands there, mist swirling around his ankles. Picture Clint Eastwood in any of his old westerns, then peel the skin away until just a memory of it covers the sharp angles, joints and bony planes of his skeleton. Dress him in black—boots, trousers, shirt. Add a Stetson and a cloak so dark, it blurs into the shadows behind him, becoming void.

Staring into that absence of light too long reminds you of every soul that ever lived and died. This sonofabitch has welcomed each and every one that stuck around in Hell with his emotionless, toothy grin.

That's Charon.

Dude's a psychopomp, a cool name from the legends of the living. Scratch that, he's *the* psychopomp. The Greeks said he ferried the dead across the Styx. Other cultures, different names, but he carried out the same purpose in all the myths. And, in every one of them, it's Charon. There's only one, like a Highlander of Death.

What function he serves in Hell puzzles me. Sure, I get

he appears when Heaven closes its gates and shuts the lights off, like a neighbor pretending they're not home when you call in unannounced, but there's nowhere to take the sorry soul that's stuck down here. Or is there?

Still, he always turns up. The baddest fucking penny ever minted. And he's showing up tonight, just to say hello? Naw, I ain't buying it.

I'm missing something about this guy, and it bugs me. He turned up at the Wheeler place last night, of course. Watching, waiting. Like the morbid, weird uncle no one wants to invite to family functions, and he sits there, sucking the life out of the room from the corner he perches in all goddamn night.

"You should have died last night, Holleran," Charon grates. His sunken, black eyes blaze with a sick fever. If the Ferryman lived, you'd call him fanatical. Or insane. "Your destiny reshaped itself five years ago, when fortune favored you. Your road came to its end in Wheeler's basement. I've known that from the very first time we met, when you cheated death. Yet here you stand, and looking at you, I see no fresh destiny. You are fateless, and this troubles me."

"Maybe you just got it wrong," I say, glancing around.

The mist grows thicker, and even Charon's breath hangs in the cold air. Didn't know the sonofabitch even breathed. That nagging sensation taps on my shoulder again, urging me to pay more attention. Something other than the Ferryman watches me. I *know* it.

"I remember you," Diana whispers, pointing at Charon. He cocks his head in her direction and nods. "You... spoke to me. After I died, but I don't remember the words."

"Most don't, child. Count yourself fortunate."

Charon turns back to me, and I'm thinking about Clint Eastwood again. Ten yards separate us, the thickening mist in between. A shoot-out at dusk. Thing is, the only weapon I could draw would do jack-shit to old Charon.

"Look," I say, throwing the Ferryman my best nonchalant shrug. Sure as Hell don't feel it. Fake it till you mean it, right? "Not my call. Lucifer intervened, and last time I looked, Hell belongs to him. You got a problem, take it up with your boss."

I hear the rip of steel before I see it. Charon glides forward a step, holding a gleaming, silver blade that shines bright against the darkness. Fuck me, but that broadsword has to be six feet long. Before I know what I'm doing, I'm standing in front of Diana, like my body could do anything 'cept get cut in half by that goddamn thing.

Charon grips the hilt in two-hands, plants the point in the ground, and leans on the pommel. If it weren't so cold, I'd sweat. Despite that dread building in my gut, gotta admit he looks like a badass.

"One day," Charon hisses, his voice like a fire that's already burned out, "Lucifer will die. Even God. I answer to no one, I existed in the void before life and all heed my call, even the Masters of Heaven and Hell."

"Diana," I whisper. Not sure why, as I'm certain Charon, the bastard, can hear anyway. "Stay close to me. This mist ain't coming from him."

"I know." Kid's already standing behind my leg, making herself small. She's smart. "I sense something. Like with the ghost on the sidewalk. Hatred, so much rage."

Curious. I add it to my mental checklist of items to

pursue later. If there *is* a goddamn later.

"You're such a dick, Charon," I snarl. Look, I'm not saying I'm not petulant sometimes, but I ain't lying either. Dude's a massive dick. "What's it matter to you if I'm alive or not? The way I see it, I'm in Hell for the long haul either way."

Charon wheezes, and it takes a while to register that I've made the creep laugh. Didn't think it possible. I fight the urge to cover my ears as his croaking continues, like the sound of gravestones rubbing together, and glance down at Diana. Her eyeless stare's fixed on the surrounding fog. At the edges of my hearing, beyond Charon's mirth, I hear growling and the padding of paws. What the fuck?

"Is that the way you see it, Nick Holleran?" the Ferryman asks. The mist swirls, soft tendrils snaking from it, wrapping around his legs. Like a caress, almost. He ignores them, the damp cold doesn't bother him. Why would it? He's Death, and blood ain't flown through his veins...ever? Still, he can breathe. I see it hanging in the air, above the mist. "You think Hell is how you perceive it? Do you believe the dead linger here for no purpose, and only where you observe them? Foolish human."

The dead serve a purpose? News to me. His thin lips unfurl from his teeth in what I reckon is a smile.

"Well, shit," I say, lifting my gun. Whatever demon's out there, I couldn't be more ill-prepared.

"What is it?" Diana asks, voice ripe with urgency and all-too alive with fear.

I nod at Charon, who's still showing me his not-so-brilliant white smile. "He knows, but he's not telling. Wants me dead so his ledger balances. Fucking oldest creature in the universe is a goddamn accountant. But, whatever it is, we need to move. Now."

"You are fateless, Nick Holleran, and you live when you should not. You cannot do that. Perhaps you will meet your demise this night after all. Be seeing you either way."

Charon steps backwards, and the mist swallows him, the fog filling in the void where he stood.

"Son of a goddamn bitch," I snarl, casting around. The night's turned white, and I've no idea where in Meadow Park we are. The Styx Bar, with Ruby and salvation, could be on the other side of the tree line, lost in the fog, just a stone's throw. Or a mile away, for all I know.

"Nick, how've you stayed alive this long?" Diana asks, voice shrill. "You just walk into danger every day?"

"Yeah, I ask myself that all the time, sweetheart."

A snarl to my right. The padding getting closer. A shape like an overgrown wolf parts the mist, silver fur dull in the consuming haze. Shards of ice jut from it like an excess of fangs. Its mouth has plenty and they're bared for me to see.

I know what it is, and that we've already met, before it even speaks.

"Time to finish what we started, Holleran," the Amarok growls.

"Really? You want to do this now? Because last time, you had a friend, and it didn't go so well for you."

There's a puddle on one of Haven's suburban streets that used to be a monster just like this one. Guess I should have expected to see the one that got away again. I just hope Charon's right about not being able to see my death.

"No Truthers to save you this time."

"Touché."

Harry and Maeve came to my rescue last night with an arcane firebomb. I'd already blown my way through my Ruger ammunition and, right now, that's all I'm packing. If we fight now, this thing'll punch my ticket quicker than I can blink.

"Diana," I grunt, backing up a step, "let's go."

"Where to?"

"Anywhere but here!"

I turn and run, and the Amarok comes pounding after me with a bloodthirsty howl. Diana glides with the grace only the dead can achieve, but I can see the fear in her face. I know all too well that even a ghost can die, and so does she. Humans don't pose a threat unless they're 'in the know', but Hell's home to many an entity that'd take pleasure turning a dead girl into an oozing pile of plasma. She's heard my business enough times over the years.

My Ruger lets a bullet fly, then another, and a third for good measure. The Amarok yelps and skids in the dirt with every impact. Only it's not just the monster I have to worry about now. The mist's thickening, almost choking. The stench of rot swims into my nostrils, makes me wanna gag.

Flesh... Fresh blood... Sweet, sweet meat... It calls to us...

The whisper snakes through the night on fingers of dread. There's a presence in the fog, closing on us all like a noose. Snuffling to my left. A loud huff of breath, like a horse getting ready to leap. Red orbs glow through the mist. The distortion makes the distance difficult to call.

I can sense their malice. Hell, I can sense the dread rolling from Diana, and even the fucking Amarok, in waves.

"Sense…" I breathe. "That's it. That's fucking it! Diana, what you said before about feeling the dead… Reach out, away from what's chasing us. Anything?"

A moment, then I hear a scream of fury, mingled with an indescribable pain, pierce through the night. Makes my fucking blood twist, and all I want to do is drop into a ball and surrender. When I glance back, the Amarok is gone, swallowed by the fog.

"A cluster. Ahead of us!" Diana starts gliding with purpose. No longer fleeing; she's leading. "It's close. Come on."

Now *I'm* following *her*. Behind me, all Hell's cutting loose. Inhuman screams—more agony than rage—tear from the fog. I charge forward and almost lose my footing as a branch snaps me across the forehead.

"Trees, you beautiful bastards. Trees!"

Trees mean the edge of the fucking park! Diana's ahead, moving without a backward glance. The fog's thinning. I plunge forward. Twigs snap beneath my feet and wet leaves slap my cheeks, but I'm alive. I'm moving and…what the Hell is that?

Something solid smashes into me. I'm knocked off my feet. Dazed, it takes me a moment to realize I'm not in danger. Haven looks near normal now that the mist is gone. Rain-slick sidewalks filled with souls. Passing cars honk and splash past as the buzz of the city comes alive around me. I sit on the wet concrete and I don't think I've ever been so glad to be lost in the grit and flair of the city's nightlife.

"Nick Holleran," the someone I collided with says.

"Hoped I'd run into you."

Nice. Gotta appreciate a well-timed quip.

"Er, hey, Jim. Sorry about that. Got a little spooked."

Jim's a skin-walker. He's in his animal form now, a coyote, and when he stands, he rises onto his hind legs like a human. Don't know how much practice went into *that*. He carries out tasks like a pro with his paws and claws, but he prefers it this way. Best of both worlds, I guess. Still wears clothes above the fur, though. A three-piece tweed suit. I'd love to know who his tailor is.

First time I laid eyes on him, I thought I'd lost my mind. Ruby had given me a nudge, reminded me how rude it is to stare. He holds out a paw and pulls me to my feet. My heart's hammering like a jackhammer, and right now, a conversation on the sidewalk's the last thing I need. Wanna run, keep going, get into The Styx and put Meadow Park behind me. But you don't just tell a skin-walker to fuck off.

"The mist," he growls. "Was that your doing?"

"No...but I had front row seats. So, you're looking for me? Kind of a coincidence. You been following me?"

Jim's tongue lolls from his mouth, flickers across his sharp teeth. He's a nice guy, but like most things in Hell, he's a dangerous one to cross.

"I said I *hoped* I'd run into you. The mist drew me here... Something familiar about it..."

He shudders, like a wet dog shaking himself, but stood upright. Wearing clothes.

Jim takes a step, stops a snout away from me. He glances at Diana, who's holding my hand. The cold runs up through my fingers into my arm. Ghosts can touch us, and we them, but I try not to. Feels like having a bucket of cold ocean thrown over you, dead fish and all. Jim turns back to me, teeth bared, and sniffs.

"We gonna have trouble, pal?"

"Why so nervous, Nick?" he snarls. To be fair, it's his only way of speaking as a coyote. "I'm smiling for Christ's sake. How've you been?"

He slaps me on the bicep with his paw, tongue lolling this way and that.

"Busy running from fog that appears out of nowhere. How about you?"

I try to step back, but he paws my wrist. I frown at him and he retracts, but steps a little closer, eyes darting around the street. This close, his scent fills my nostrils. Reminds me of cinnamon.

"About that... Lots of weird things in Hell lately. You heard about those Wendigo sightings?"

"Yeah," I reply, keeping my distance. If Jim ever heard of personal space, he isn't a fan, that's for sure. Folk stream past us, normal humans oblivious as usual, some instinct whispering at them, telling them to give us all a wide berth. They don't see who I'm talking to, who's clutching my hand. "I hear a lot of things, you know?"

"My clan's getting nervous. Skin-walkers and Wendigo are blood enemies, Nick. We're peaceful folk; heck, most of the stories that paint us as the bad guys are because of Wendigo. But they're in *packs*, man. That's unheard of. A group of them would tear each other apart without hesitation. If you ask me, something stinks. Will you look into it, see what's got them stirred up?"

I remember Ruby telling me about Wendigo just yesterday. Come to think of it, Harry mentioned them to me earlier in the week. He took a special interest in them. Twenty-four hours ago, he'd have been my first port of call. Boy, am I gonna miss his expertise. And his friendship.

Wendigo are bad news; they're malevolent spirits that possess all manner of creatures—animal, human and demon. I've only read about them, heard stories from Harry. I've never had the pleasure of coming face-to-face with one. Yet.

"They attacked any of your people?"

"No, but it's only a matter of time, I fear. Surprised they haven't. They hate us. Not that they don't hate *most* things. But their focus on us seems personal. Wish I knew why. The Elders know, but they won't say. I fought one once. Thought I was finished. Those eyes... They still haunt my dreams. A Wendigo possessing a skin-walker... Nick, it's an abomination. Makes my skin itch just thinking about it."

I glance at Diana and smile. "Look, Jim. Got a couple of matters to attend to. Leave some details with Ruby next time you're in The Styx and I'll nose around, see what turns up, yeah? Best I can do right now."

Jim scratches at the fur behind one of his ears, makes me wanna do that same. I can't help but picture fleas hopping from his fur right onto me. "Guess that'll have to do. Talk soon, Nick. Keep your wits about you. Hell's restless."

"Tell me something I don't know," I mutter, itching the back of my neck as he stalks away. Diana's still gripping my hand. "You okay, kid?"

"How can you live here, with all this around you?"

"You can get used to anything, I guess. Come on. We're almost there. Then we can take a load off and catch up."

Diana's pits focus on Meadow Park again. The fog lingers behind the tree line, but it's silent now. Across the sidewalk, some washed-out ghosts are looking that way too. They're Aware, and I'm sure they heard the screams, saw me charging full-tilt into poor, old Jim. One of them glances my way, worry lines clear on her forehead even from this distance. Her name's Suzy. She's a riot, but the park's got her worried.

Me too, sister.

"Come on," I say to Diana, rubbing the back of my neck again. "Think I got whiplash. That building's where we're headed. The Styx."

"This place, is it safe?" she asks, and I'm reminded of how young she is. Girl's dead all of fifty-six years, but she's still a teenager.

"Styx's safer than Meadow Park," I say, dodging slow-moving cars as we cross over the road. "Gotta be."

"You sure? You don't seem very popular, Nick."

Fair point.

"Don't worry. Ruby's like me, but she's had this curse a lot longer than I have. She's a survivor, and she runs The Styx for people like us who have to live with all this. She founded the place in the late-70s, warded the stones with serious runes to keep the worst of Haven away from its doors, and I don't know about you, but that appeals right now. She welcomes all entities of Hell, just so long as we behave. Ruby doesn't suffer fools, and she's got house rules. Follow them, and the place is like a second home. Don't, and..." I remember the demon, Cyril, pinning me to the wall. Suraz, decapitating him. "...it can get messy. But I'm not planning on breaking any of her rules tonight. Are you?"

She shakes her head, but even without eyes she manages to look pensive.

"This place'll work for you, kid. It's a great place to mingle, meet people like you, learn how things work. And they serve a mean piña colada. Honest. They're delicious."

We're halfway to The Styx's front door when my heart sinks like the Titanic. Outside the bar's entrance, leaning against the wall, is an obsidian-skinned Nephilim. One of the two that call Haven home. His raven hair flows to his waist and the melancholy in his eyes engulfs me when he spots me. I'm crushed by the weight of an eternity of regret, spliced with anger, though a part of me recognizes it isn't as heavy as having Lucifer stood in front of you. I won't forget that experience in a hurry.

"Come the fuck on."

I even throw in a groan for good measure, like the overgrown teenager I sometimes am.

"Nick Holleran," Suraz booms, voice thumping inside my skull. "You ignored my advice. I warned you to tread with care. Instead, I learn you've fought Amarok, dragged two Truthers into your feud with Wheeler, walked into the middle of a ritual to bind the Devil, and met Lucifer himself. Now, I find you running around Hell with an newly Aware ghost like nothing has happened. Do you have a death wish?"

Before I can answer, Suraz launches forward, grabs the lapels of my jacket in a thick fist and drags me into The Styx.

CARRY THAT WEIGHT

Now and then, the fates align and I understand keeping my big mouth shut is a fabulous idea. When a pissed Nephilim hauls me into The Styx by the collar, my instincts inform me that, yes, this is one of those times.

Suraz leaves me by the entrance and storms off behind the bar, through the door downstairs to where the real action happens. The barkeep on this floor, Guz, does his best to pretend a seething Nephilim ain't just stomped by. Gotta appreciate the man's decision not to get involved. I know I sure as Hell wouldn't.

A bunch of posters hang behind the bar, mostly for bands that play at The Styx, the Tomb of Nick Cage amongst them. Now that's music the living and the dead can appreciate. Except that today, plastered over the top of their flyers, are missing posters. Dozens of posters for cats, dogs, even horses.

Huh. Those weren't there yesterday.

I glance at Diana. Her eyeless sockets peer up at me, but I'm getting swell at reading her face. Right now, it says, *What the Hell have you got me into?*

"All's well," I murmur to her, throwing her a small

smile, even though my stomach's churning. "Suraz is just... passionate."

Diana covers her ears as the band on stage slams into action. The Styx has two levels. The living, unaware as ever, hang around upstairs, oblivious to the fact that below them is a hive for Haven's demonic and ghostly population. It's funny; the place draws a crowd who're into the occult, arcane, horror films and Stephen King books, like they *sense* what the place is, but don't have the awareness to see what surrounds them.

Terrible music, though.

The bands that play here all have names like Mr. Urine, Cow Annihilation, and Toxic Puke. They're masters in creating horrific, dirge-like cacophonies and the Goths love it. I'm watching the bass player, hearing nothing but the drone of crunching guitar, and I wonder if he even knows why he's there. The track doesn't have even the slightest bounce of a bass line. A million miles away from The Beatles, and I'm pretty sure Diana is missing Nirvana right about now.

"Nick, what the fuck have you done this time?"

I jump before I can stop myself. After Diana, Charon and the park, my nerves are shot. Pink-haired Ruby, owner of The Styx and barkeep downstairs, glares at me now that she has my attention. Look, she has to shout so I can hear her over the goddamn noise of Sludge Hammer or whatever these punks call themselves, but by the look on her face, I reckon she'd scream bloody murder at me even if we stood in a library.

We usually get along, but events last night involved me in the death of her best customer. I took a case a while back that took a nasty turn. Cyril's familiar, Francis, searched for a way to summon Lucifer—seems like it's the thing to do in Haven at the moment—and ended up sacrificing a number of poor teenage girls to do it. I Expunged him. Didn't have a choice. Expunction doesn't just mean death; it means total eradication. It's a Hell of a punishment, but Francis deserved it.

Cyril took exception, and wanted my head. Guess I understood. Demon familiars don't just love each other. It runs way deeper than that. Their connection's on an elemental level, and I'd scrubbed Francis from the tapestry of existence. So, we got into a ruckus, and Cyril lost *his* head. In my defense, I didn't deliver the killing blow—Suraz did—and I *did* help clean up the mess.

"Nothing," I yell back, spreading my hands wide, "honest. Nephilim grabbed me on the sidewalk and yanked me in here."

"Huh," Ruby fumes, before glancing at Diana, who looks like she wants to sink into the floor. I wonder if she can? "Who's this?"

A line of living, ghosts and demons file out of the basement door, many ashen-faced. More so than usual, I might add, which takes some doing when you're talking about the dead.

"What's going on?" I ask, ignoring her question.

Ruby scowls. "Suraz crashed through the door and told us all to get out. Took one look at his face and agreed. Then I saw you and put the story together. Of *course* it had to be Nick fucking Holleran. Again. You gonna make me ask twice?"

I glance at Diana. She's standing as close to me as possible. Poor girl. I really shoulda taken her somewhere else to talk, but I'd run outta options. Cops outside my apartment, murder scene in my office, Charon and fog monsters in the park. This is all too much for her, and my head ain't screwed on right. I've no idea how to look after a kid, alive or not, and in a moment of divine clarity, I understand this case she charged me with involves just that. She's a child, alone in Hell, and I'm the closest thing to a responsible adult she has.

Well, shit...

"A client. She. Is. A. Client!" I shout over another passage of crunching guitar and screaming from the 'vocalist' in the band. "I came here so we could talk. I didn't know Suraz would be waiting on me. I'll bring you up to speed later, yeah?"

From the corner of my eye, I see a ghost approaching, Luis is his name. He's sheepish and a nice enough sort. Told me one time he reckoned he didn't get into Heaven because he never went to church, said the frescos freaked him out. From what I've learned, God's fickle enough to use that as a reason, but I'm sure a fella as shifty as him's hiding all kinds of skeletons.

"Ah, Nick?" he mutters, wide eyes darting everywhere and nowhere. "The Nephilim wants you downstairs."

"No shit," I deadpan. Think I'm feeling a little better. My smart-ass side's returning. "Come on, Diana. Let's see what Suraz has to say."

"Are you in trouble?"

She doesn't move. The folks Suraz evicted stare at us, a mixture of speculation and concern on their faces. Kid's shit scared, and I can't say I blame her.

"No." The reassuring smile I give her makes my cheek muscles throb. "Me and the Nephilim go way back. Just a misunderstanding, is all. We'll straighten things out, then me and you'll talk shop. Don't worry, sweetheart, Suraz is..."

We walk through the door, and the words 'a teddy bear' die on my lips. The Nephilim stands in the room's center, black wings spread, mighty golden broadsword planted point-first in the ground. He's an obsidian terror, teeth bared, yellow eyes narrowed. I look away from the bright red blood on his blade, then notice he has it splashed on his black armor and face.

"... pissed," I finish, with a sigh.

The Nephilim holds up his mighty fist, unfurls a single finger and points right at me.

"What do you have to say for yourself, Nick Holleran? You have one life left. Should you act with such recklessness?"

I can't look at him. The weight of his glare is too much. It feels like powerlessness, but tenfold. A kind of waking sleep paralysis, trapped inside the dead weight of your body, mind screaming, begging you to do *something*, but it just won't do as it's told. Suraz's voice thunders in my head, pushing my skull to breaking point. I want to sink to my knees, but that stubborn, pig-headed streak's latched onto something, and I can't help myself.

Hey, it shouldn't surprise me. Curiosity got me killed once already.

"Why do you give a shit?" I growl. "There's millions of souls in Haven, living and dead. Hell, there's a bunch of folk who can *see* just like me upstairs."

My eyeballs throb like invisible needles are sinking into them. Despite what I said to reassure the kid before, me and the Nephilim have shared a handful of words in five years. A slice of advice over a drink last night's one thing. This level of ferocity is something else altogether, and my flesh ain't happy with me fighting against Suraz's will.

"The Devil didn't break God's laws for any of them, Holleran."

"Ah," I say, pieces sliding together as I stare at a point beside his face. It's better than looking in his eyes. The hammer trying to split my skull becomes just a little less insistent. "So that's what has you all riled up. You've spoken to him, the Devil? Interesting."

The thump of the band upstairs fills the silence between us. Then, with a petulant toss of his head that sends his raven hair flowing, Suraz slams his sword into its sheath and his wings fold against his back. The weight threatening to crush me eases, and I hear Diana whisper in relief. She felt it too, maybe more than I did.

"Yes," Suraz says, shoulders sagging a little, like the anger pouring from him has left his limbs weak. "After his encounter with you."

"There's more to this," Diana whispers, at my side. She's trembling. "He's hurting. So much sadness now the rage has gone."

If Suraz heard, he doesn't show it.

"Look," I say, spreading my hands. "I didn't *ask* Lucifer to heal me. Quite the opposite. I'd made my peace, but he did his own thing. Who am I to argue? You should thank me. From what Lucifer says, I spared him from some nasty business. Heard Wheeler could have extracted all kinds of binding promises from him."

Suraz strides towards me, and halts a sword's-reach away. Between him and Charon, I'm getting pretty damn sick of swords tonight. I force myself to look him in the eye, and Goddamn, if it isn't one of the hardest things I've ever done. My brain's boiling and I'm surprised there's no steam pumping from my ears.

I see the sorrow as his stare penetrates me. I've seen Absin a few times and she has that look too. It figures. Heaven is a perfect existence, they say. Sure, Suraz and her chose to follow Lucifer in the fight against God, but they lost, wound up exiled. Never to return.

Nothing can compare to the life they had before. Thing is, I get the feeling Suraz's sadness runs deeper than that, more personal.

The Nephilim nods. It's a grudging acknowledgement.

"I am aware of this, and I appreciate your selflessness. Though it benefits you little. Heaven is closed to you." Suraz frowns and looks away. "As it is to me."

I wanna ask a question, but Diana throws me a gesture that, despite the age gap, I can interpret as 'shut the fuck up'. She glides forward, like she's attached to an invisible string leading to the Nephilim and reaches out to him, takes his hand in hers. Suraz blinks. A look of shock passes across his face when they make contact. He kneels in front of her, eyes to sockets.

In complete silence, the Nephilim stares deep into her small face, and whatever passes between them isn't for me to know.

The moment stretches until Suraz smiles—a fucking smile from the Nephilim of all things—and caresses Diana's cheek with a fingertip.

"She is a rare one," he says, looking up at me. I gotta admit, having one of Lucifer's Goddamn archangels kneeling in front of me with a serene smile plastered on his face is a sight I'm not prepared for. "You are helping her move on?"

It's my turn to blink. The endgame with Diana's case hadn't occurred to me until now. When I discover her killer, she'll get closure and move on, if God allows it. Children are innocent, so he's got to, right? Despite only talking for the first time tonight, Diana represents the one constant thing in my second life: the ghost in the corner from day one. Not sure I'm ready to say goodbye to that.

"I guess. Yeah, I mean, that's the case, right? Closure."

Suraz climbs to his feet, Diana still holding his hand. "I see you attract trouble, Nick Holleran, but your cause is noble. Watch yourself. You should have died twice already, Lucifer grants few mortals the same chances as you. Hell stirs, human, and you stand at the center of its unrest. This I know, and so do others. See to the girl, but take care. Forces beyond your comprehension are making their move, and they will not hesitate to end you if you get in their way."

He releases his hold on Diana and pats her on her tiny head. Giving me one last, hard stare, he strides by.

"Gee, thanks," I mumble, then a thought pops into my head. "Wait!"

Suraz pauses, his back to me. There's something I gotta ask him. The question of why Hell's the way it is, with humans living beside the dead, has plagued me these last five years. Last night, the Devil handed me a nugget of truth.

"Lucifer told me that we *all* lived in Heaven. That the humans joined his rebellion, and God cast us all out. That right?"

"Yes." Suraz's shoulders sag again. "He... We...fought for you, though your kind do not remember. For God's angels, Heaven represented perfection. That bliss did not extend to everyone."

"So God just created this whole place to punish us, like Lucifer said. What about Charon? He created him too?"

The Nephilim spins on his heel, finger pointing my way again.

"These are dangerous questions, and ones you would do well to forget, Holleran. One life left."

He sweeps from the room, leaving me with more questions and no notion to stop asking them.

"Let's get a table," I say to Diana. "We got some talking to do."

...

I put myself into Diana's shoes as the bar returns to normal around us. The folk Suraz evicted slink back in and get on with their night like nothing happened. All except Ruby, who's eyeing me something awful, but she brought me over an Old Fashioned and put it on my tab.

Bob, a dead guitarist, is back on stage, strumming his acoustic. Some say he died there and never stopped playing. I wonder if his last name's Johnston, and if he sold his soul to... Wait, what am I thinking?

Weariness is prodding me. My body's remembering the punishment it's taken over the last twenty-four hours now that Lucifer's shot of vitality is wearing off. I hoped I'd make the night, but all the excitement since leaving my office is catching up with me.

Diana sits across from me, an untouched glass of paint-stripper on the table. It ain't *real* paint-stripper, but it sure tastes like it. See, ghosts have vices like the living and some enjoy getting 'wasted', but alcohol for the living won't cut it. Not strong enough, not by a long shot. So Ruby serves them a concoction made up of medicinal alcohol, powerful spirits that should never get mixed, and Lucifer knows what else.

I move the glass away from Diana. Not sure why Ruby poured it for the kid. Even though she's dead, she's underage. Force of habit, I reckon.

Diana stumps me. She sprang Awareness and Strengthened pretty much overnight. She can walk, talk and affect the rest of Hell, and interact however she wants, plus this whole 'empathy' thing. Never seen *that* before. Why'd that happen now? Why so quick?

But I gotta understand what it's like for her. The kid woke up in the office where her murderer took her eyes and did God knows what else to her. I take her on a sojourn through Hell, where we're waylaid by Charon, creatures in the mist and a fucking Nephilim.

So, I smile, and I keep it simple.

"Rough hour, huh? Tell me about yourself, kid."

What else can I say? I'm an only child and I lost my folks young. Mommy *and* daddy issues hover like a ghost in the corner of an office. I spent most of my childhood alone, so I've no experience talking to kids, let alone dead ones born almost two decades before me.

She throws a little furtive look around, attention settling on a table close by. A dead couple sits at it, talking away without a care in the world. Donny and Beth died in a climbing accident ten years back and wound up staying in Hell. Nice couple.

A frown forms as I wonder what's so interesting about them. Maybe it's how they're sitting on a solid chair, but then so's the kid. Hell's like that. The ghosts can interact with anything. It's their plane of existence, just like ours, so why shouldn't they?

Then it hits me. Donny's Korean, Beth's black.

"It's all so different," Diana breathes, lips curving into a whisper of a smile. "A black gal sitting in a bar with her fella who don't look like her."

"Things have changed," I reply, my fingers itching to pull out a cigarette. Instead, I take a sip of the Old Fashioned, deciding I can do without Diana's thoughts on smoking. "We're moving on from all that. Or we're trying our damned best, at least. Sure, there's still pockets of assholes spouting bull, but we're mending what can be mended and we keep on trying. It ain't always perfect, but we're getting there. That's what I tell myself, anyway. A white dude who's never had someone scream in *my* face about the color of *my* skin."

"They love each other so much," Diana says, as if she didn't hear a word I said. "Can't you feel it?"

I glance over my shoulder at Donny and Beth and shrug.

"I can *see* it. The way they're staring into each other's eyes, all moony-like."

"What about you, Nick? You said you'd talk to Rosa about your date."

Laughter bubbles up from my chest, and I shake my head. "We're talking about you? Who're you, anyway? Cupid?"

She gives me a small shrug, attention still locked on the love-ghosts. "I know how you feel about her. All those emotions jumbling around when you think about Rosa. You ain't gonna solve them by pushing her away, mister."

"Fine," I sigh, pulling out my cell. Diana's intuition with emotion and feeling interests me. It should. Saved my bacon tonight, no doubt. She sensed the cluster of souls gathered here, and picked out a path through Meadow Park to The Styx. Man, bet that pisses old Charon off. "I'll send her a message, see if we can bump our date up. Then can we talk about you?"

She nods. "Sure, Nick."

I send Rosa a message. As has become my mantra tonight, I keep it simple.

Hey, I know I said next week, but I'm free tomorrow. Sound good?

"Right, done. This empathy you have. It's not new, is it? I'm asking since you don't seem surprised by it."

Diana turns to face me, and I fight the urge to look away from where her eyes used to be. Instead, I picture her *with* eyes and smile back. It ain't her fault she looks the way she does, and me acting all childish when she stares my way won't do her any favors.

"I guess I could always do it a little. It's why I helped momma so well with the babies. I *knew* how they felt before they did."

"World's a weird and wonderful place." I take a sip of my drink, considering my next words. My mind's running slow. Fuck, I'm tired. "Still, bet your talent had its drawbacks."

Diana shrinks in her seat and gives a small nod. "I knew when people felt angry. More than mad. The man who ki... Well, I don't ever want to feel like that again. Rage, terror, shame, pleasure, regret. All rolled into one."

An Empath. Neat trick, but a tough one for a child to possess.

"Kid, I have to say this and I hate it, but you need to understand. The monster who killed you, fair chance he's dead. If he's your unfinished business, then you'll have to let him go."

Diana shakes her head. "No, he's alive, Nick. I know it. He wasn't all that older than me. Twenty, maybe. Twenty-one."

"White, I'm guessing."

"Yeah."

"I can call in a few favors. Reckon a good place to start is pulling up records on who used to live in my office. That might take a day or two. The other angle is *your* family. Diana, you said you've got younger siblings. *They* could still be around. Tell me about them."

Diana grins, and my heart breaks just a little. Look, I don't try to make out I have a heart of stone. Emotion doesn't make me wanna run a marathon in the opposite direction, but the look of hope on her little face makes me uncomfortable.

"Could, I said, kid. *Could.*"

That tempers the smile somewhat, and I feel like a dick.

"We lived in the projects over on Redwood and Maine. Daddy taught us; he educated all the kids round our way. He said he taught himself letters and how to speak proper. Even still, Daddy might have been the smartest man I knew. Made me read a new book each week. Not the kids' ones neither. Science-fiction from H. G. Wells, mysteries from Doyle. Polio took him when I turned ten. That left me, Momma, Gloria, Stacey, Florence and Mary. I worked in the diner and the Laundromat, and I'd just started at a bar, cleaning glasses at night. It's there I met *him.*" She points at her face. "The one who did this. I'd seen him, the only white man in the joint, for about a week before he took me."

"How long did he..." I start, then grimace. "Look, there's no skirting this. Did he kill you right away?"

For a moment, I'm thinking she won't answer. Glancing around, I see the place has filled up. There's a crowd at the bar, but Ruby's still looking my way.

"He made me stand in the corner, staring at the wall." My attention jerks back to Diana. Her voice is shaking, about to break. "It made him furious if I even glanced at him in the corner of my eyes. That's why he took them before he..."

I reach out and put my hand over hers. The coldness sends a shiver snaking through my body. Like I said, it's something I avoid if I'm able, but Diana's crying invisible tears, small body shaking from her sobs, and she's only got me to console her.

Some folk get all the luck, huh?

"Hey, kid. It's in the past. He can't hurt you now." Hollow words, and I know it. Memories haunt harder than any ghost I've met in Hell. She only just stopped reliving the moment of her death. "Redwood and Maine. Can't say I'm familiar, but we can check it out. Let's say I take you home, and we'll pick up the case tomorrow."

"Your office? No, Nick. Don't take me back there, please!"

The fierceness of her voice startles me. I raise my hands, like I'm trying to calm a wild mustang. No office then. Cops can't stay outside my place all day and night, can they?

Well, maybe they can, but we need to go *somewhere*.

"Okay, kid. We don't have to go there. My apartment, how's that sound?"

Diana nods, settling down a little. In my peripheral vision, I see Ruby making her way over. I'm light-headed, not from drink but tiredness. I'm bone-deep exhausted.

"One thing, Diana. When we find this sonofabitch, what do you want?"

Her eyeless stare pins me. "I want him to know it's me who's come for him. I want to see him beg."

I open my mouth to reply, to warn the kid about revenge, but Ruby interrupts me.

"So, you want to tell me who this lovely, little lady is before you cause another fight in my place? There's *still* demon ichor stuck between the floorboards, Nick."

"Ruby, Diana. Diana, Ruby. Now we're all friends.

Kid's the one I've shared an office with for the last half-decade. She's got a case for me."

Ruby's eyes narrow. "Is that all? Just another case?"

"Diana became Aware tonight. Turns out she's been half-listening to me yammer on for years. Ain't that right, kid?"

She just nods, head down.

"Coincidence, I'm sure," Ruby says, in a tone that suggests it's anything but. Not sure I believe it either. Maybe Lucifer left his mark on me and that woke the kid up. Ruby points over my shoulder. "Anyway, there's a guy who came in asking for you while you had your business with Suraz. He's sitting by the stage. He's not dead, so I'm pretty sure he's one of us. Why don't you go and chat, and I'll get to know our little friend here?"

The room spins and takes its sweet time settling when I look around. I needed my bed as soon as I left the Wheelers' place last night. I squint and make out a heavy-set man with a face like the moon—pale, round and hairless.

"Huh."

I don't recognize him, and now I'm wondering what business he has with me. I've already picked up two new cases tonight. I don't need another.

Diana's smiling up at Ruby and she's smiling back. If anyone can make the kid feel at home in Hell, it's her.

"You two have fun now. Don't talk about me too much."

"There's something about that man..." Diana says, glancing over at the fella who's nursing his untouched drink. "He's...familiar, somehow."

"Guess he must have one of those faces," I smile. "You're safe with Ruby, kid. Relax. I'll be right back."

She nods as I get up and Ruby slides into my seat. I hear them start chatting right away.

A smile breaks out across the stranger's face as I approach, and he raises a thick hand in salute. I scowl, because that smile ain't touching his eyes. They're cold and flat. Killer's eyes, peering out of a placid, dull face. I'm edgy right away, but my brain's working too slow. You know when you're beat, and your head's filled with wool? My entire body's like that. I'm moving my limbs but they don't *feel* like they belong to me. They're these weird, floating appendages with a fuggy mind of their own.

"Strange weather we're having, friend," he says, voice deep but flat, almost monotonous. He reaches his hand out. I don't take it.

"Yeah," I say, giving him the once over. "You can say that again."

Guy's tall. I can tell even with him sitting down. He's bigger than me by a round, bald head, and I ain't no small fry. He smiles up at me with those shark eyes. I suppress a shudder. He's low-key freaking me out, and it's not just the oddness of *those* eyes in *that* face. There's a vibe around him I don't like.

"Rain and heat one minute, cold mists the next."

"You've got a case for me?" I ask, giving him a small, tight smile and cutting to the chase. "What's your name, pal? Since it seems you know mine already, but we haven't been introduced."

"It's a pleasure to meet you, Mr. Holleran. I'm Marvin Clancy."

I feel the frown forming. Something swirls inside those black eyes. Joy? No. More than that. Adulation, like all those pictures of teenage girls mooning at The Beatles when they came to America. Thanks, Diana, for the handy reference point. My heart's hammering inside my chest. Because of the weariness catching up to me, or is it him?

"Do I know you?"

Folk say I'm a touch too direct at times.

"Unfortunately not, Mr. Holleran. I'm looking for my dog. The news reports state they have a habit of going missing of late, and I fear the worst. I came into The Styx to drop in a poster, and I thought I might speak with you. I saw you hauled in here, if I can beg your pardon for the phrase," he pauses, his tongue snakes out like a fat, red slug and runs across his lips, "by the Nephilim."

I need to sit down before I fall, though my gut's screaming at me to get the fuck away from this guy as soon as I can.

"Marv..." My brain whispers to me, tells me to draw my Ruger. Without agreeing, my fingers inch their way to the holster under my coat. I tell them to fucking stop. Maybe it's my shot nerves, maybe paranoia or some intuition, but the shadow I thought moved in my office window pops into my head. "Cut the shit. This ain't about no dog. Are you following me?"

"I'm sorry, Mr. Holleran. It does appear that way, doesn't it? You are blessed to have the privilege to speak with one such as the Nephilim, and others greater than he." Sweat's beading on his thick forehead. "Take a seat, please."

"Rather stand," I reply, trying to keep from swaying.

My legs are about to give out, but I'm way too stubborn to change my mind now.

Anger flashes in those charcoal eyes, and his kind face turns hard, like granite. Just for a second.

"Have it your way," Marv purrs, all smiles again. "I've heard of you, of course. I'm like you. Well, perhaps I over-estimate myself there. Let's just say, I can *see.* I have desired to make your acquaintance for some time. The Nephilim's interest confirmed my need."

"What in Hell are you talking about?"

Marv reeks of bullshit. I can 'see' pretty well myself and I'm peering straight through this front he's putting on. Marvin Clancy makes my teeth itch.

"He's left his mark on you." The way he says 'he', it's like he's talking about a lover. He closes his eyes, slug-like tongue sliding over his lips. Still sweating. I wanna gag. "I can taste it. You're blessed by the Devil, aren't you, Mr. Holleran? You have basked in His presence, felt His power. I know what you do, how you help the living and the dead. I would like to offer you a job."

I look over my shoulder at Diana and Ruby but they ignore me, deep in conversation. It's a mistake. The room lurches when I turn back to Marv. I lean on his table, my face close to his. His eyes search my face, filled with that adulation again, and I decide that, whenever the dude died and returned, it broke him.

"My diary's pretty full, Marv. Just took on a fresh case. Two, as a matter of fact. Maybe some other time."

"Maybe. Or maybe your two cases are more connected than you think. Maybe my case is connected too. Isn't that how it works in detective novels, Mr. Holleran?"

"I wish my life was that simple."

"I can offer you simplicity. Money is no object."

When I hear that, my ears dance. Might be my favorite sentence. I could get hitched and settle down with those four words. They could have my last name, no problem. *Money is no object, Holleran.* Has a ring to it.

Granted, I have a ten thousand dollar check in my office drawer that I refuse to cash. The claret might be mine, but it's blood money and there are strings attached somewhere. So money's tight and, normally, I'd jump at the chance for quick cash. Still, there's something about Marv that makes my skin crawl, and even in this exhausted, addled state, I ain't broke enough to take his green.

"Thanks for the offer."

I make to leave, but his meaty hand shoots out with impossible speed, and fastens around my wrist like a vise.

"You've the Devil's mark, Holleran." Desperation in his voice, anger on his face. "Long have I desired to speak with Him, to bathe in His glorious presence, His glory. Summon Him for me. Fifty thousand dollars."

My lips curl in disgust. Pulling my coat back, I rest my other hand on my Ruger.

"A Devil Worshipper, huh?" I spit.

There's plenty of those folk in Hell. Some are harmless—regular, misguided people who don't know shit and think the Devil hides messages on Black Sabbath vinyls and dresses up at Halloween. And some are dangerous.

I'd bet Marv's 50k he's one of the latter. See, Lucifer isn't *bad*, as I discovered myself just last night. He's different and he's *in*different. Mortals can't hope to understand him. Devil Worshippers who can *see*, they're trouble. Sick in the soul. Obsessed with 'Satan'. Let's just say I've spent a lot of time tracking down folk like Marvin Clancy for the most heinous acts anyone could imagine. Their kind pop up with alarming consistency these days.

"Back the fuck off, or you're leaving this place in a bag. And don't think dying will protect you. I know what to do with ghosts who cause trouble, let me tell you."

Marv bares his teeth in a grin, but his eyes remain untouched. There's no adulation now, just Ted Bundy malice and hunger.

"You have made a mistake, Mr. Holleran," he says, releasing me. His fingers have left their mark on my wrist. "A grave mistake."

He climbs to his feet and looks down at me. He's pretty fucking tall. Sometimes, I hate being right.

"Be seeing you."

Charon said that exact same thing. *Be seeing you.*

I watch him over my shoulder as he leaves, only taking my hand away from the Ruger when he disappears up the stairs. I sigh, and a wave of weariness washes over me. I rub at my temples. Time for bed. Way past time.

"Diana?" I call, turning her way. I keep twisting, but now The Styx spins too. I hear a yell—mine—as I crash facefirst onto a table and into darkness.

A LITTLE HELP FROM MY FRIENDS

It takes about two seconds after I open my eyes for the pain to catch up.

I don't know which part of my body to hold, so I make do with lying and mewling like a newborn lamb. At least the bed's soft.

Wait. Bed?

It hurts to turn my head, but I do it anyway. Sunlight streams through half-drawn window blinds, assaulting my eyes in the process, and illuminates the bedroom of my cramped, low-rent apartment. Weird things happen in Hell all the time, but I sure as shit didn't teleport here. Someone brought me home, and that means the cops must have taken off. That, or I'm under house arrest.

I try to say, 'hello?' but a hacking cough rips into life instead. It rattles the ribs that were broken just yesterday, and the tortured flesh around the point where Michelle Wheeler jammed a knife in my side. My head starts to pound like a kick drum, striking up the rest of the band. I feel like someone's grabbed me around the neck and shredded my spine for a guitar solo.

Lucifer's healing must be like going under the knife.

Fine until the pain meds wear off. He's fused my ribs back together, and I ain't leaking blood from Michelle's killing plunge, but Lord above does it hurt.

"Think I'd rather have died," I mutter, and then, because you never know who's listening, "I'm kidding."

I'm lucky to be alive. I appreciate that in a way I haven't in a while. Maybe it was the promise of Heaven that made me long for death once, but pretty quick I fell into this lethargy instead. Cynicism, some might say. I know Rosa said it often, but change is in the air. Events at the Wheelers' saw to that. And the kid? She needs my help.

Just as soon as I can stand.

I decide against trying it just yet and let the mattress hold me. Room's nice. Ain't too hot or cold and the sheets are soft. Which I'm feeling in a pretty holistic way right about now. Frowning, I peak under the sheets and discover I'm buck-ass naked.

I've woken up in stranger situations but, still, it's unnerving. Casting my mind back's like wading through a river of molasses, but the immediate events from the night before replay. I recall the conversation with Diana, the look in Marvin Clancy's eyes before he left The Styx, the table rushing up to greet my face.

"Be seeing you," I whisper. Charon said the same thing. Funny turn of phrase, that. Sticks in the mind.

I'm not a big enough fool to think I've seen the last of either of them.

Voices drift in from the other room, and I mean literally 'the other room.' My apartment has two—the bedroom with its en suite, and the den with its open-plan kitchen. I don't need much and spend little time here. It never felt like home and I can't say anywhere has, not since I came back the first time. For a place to sleep, it'll do. It's close to my office and overlooks the corner of Chessington and Fox, a stone's throw from The Styx.

I sit up, listening harder to the conversation. Two women—Diana and Ruby—and I can't hear what they're saying, but they sound like they're getting along. That's just swell. I could almost relax, except another stab of pain rips into my side.

My cell pings. Fumbling for it, I see someone—Ruby, I'd guess—charged it and placed it next to my pillow. Quality service. I should leave her a tip. Squinting, I check the screen and find a message from Rosa.

Up late last night, Nick? Some things don't change. I can meet tonight. 8pm, I'll get us a table at Tony's. You're paying.

The cell drops from my fingers as a wave of weariness takes me. I don't know why Rosa keeps hanging around, waiting for me to sort my shit out, but the message raises a smile. At ease, I sink into sleep for a little longer. Hell can wait.

...

Hammering on the front door and muffled yells jerk me awake, set my heart pounding. Ruby sticks her pink-haired head into my bedroom.

"Nick, wake up. It's the cops."

"Shit." I swing a bare leg out of bed and pause. Ruby's still watching. "You mind?"

She rolls her eyes. "You've got nothing I haven't seen before, Nick. Who d'you think put you to bed last night, sugar?"

Scowling, I improvise and wrap the bed sheet around me, like some pauper Roman Emperor. Or like I'm at a frat party. "Fine, just stay in here while I talk to them."

She moves aside as I push by her, but I see the concern in her eyes. Ruby's someone I can rely on and she knows I don't have the best relationship with the local PD. Not to say I'm at odds with all of them. I've had a run-in once or twice, but most remember my days working with the department, and the rest think I'm a crank.

As I leave the bedroom, I realize I haven't brought Ruby up to speed on the events at the Wheeler place, not to mention Harry and Maeve's passing. I'll add it to my to-do list.

Diana's stood by the front door, watching the frame rattle and shake as the cops bang on it. She glances at me, and I nod to the bedroom. It's not like the cops will notice her, but I don't want the distraction.

Like I said, I've a couple of allies, but this isn't them. I saw the car parked out front yesterday, and the people friendly with me like to keep a distance. Drawing in a deep breath and fixing a sleepy smile on my face, I open the door a crack and, even though I guessed who's come to shake me down, I deflate like a popped balloon. Officers Butler and Gavin ain't my friends. Quite the opposite.

"Damn, Lori," Henry Butler smirks, nudging his partner. "Kind of ironic, right? Haven's foremost Paranormal Investigator sleeps like the fucking dead."

"Give him a break, Henry," she says, trying to peer past me into my apartment. "Maybe he's got a ghost in there. How about it, Holleran? Doing some pro bono work for the stiffs?"

I glance over my shoulder. Diana's eyeless stare meets mine as she backs into my bedroom. "I like to catch the ones that slip through the net. Y'know, the ones the system fails."

"Funny guy," Henry says. "But then, you're just one big joke, ain't ya?"

"You want to do this on the doorstep, Nick, or can we come in?" Lori asks.

"Want to do what? You're not here on police business or you'd have a warrant."

"Come on, Nick," Henry chides, sticking his foot in the door, "don't be an ass."

"Yeah. We just swung by to catch up. We were starting to worry. Didn't see you here or at your office all day yesterday. Me and Henry, we're doing our civic duty, checking up on Haven's one-and-only Paranormal Investigator. I mean, where would we be if something happened to you? Whole city would go to Hell."

I snort. Look, I don't know what the problem is with these clowns. They don't like me, and I'm not too fond of them. Fact of the matter is, these bastards are waiting for me to slip up, and right now, I've got the nagging feeling, a memory tapping me on the shoulder, begging for my attention, that I'm missing something real important.

"Appreciate the concern," I say, opening the door a touch wider so they can see my bed sheet chic. "But I just woke up. It's been a rough couple of days."

Henry doesn't seem impressed. Lori gives me a slow up-and-down. I flash her my lopsided grin in return. She scowls when she meets my eye. I'm holding out on that boyish charm working one of these day.

"Rough couple of days, huh?" Henry bites out through gritted teeth, his animosity palpable. "Then you'll be glad to know the HPD's looking out for you in your hour of need. These rough days have anything to do with a case, Nick? How'd it turn out?"

It starts as a chill at the bottom of my spine, then splits and spreads across my body. I'm hyper-aware and weak all at the same time.

Fear.

I've remembered what I've forgotten, the events I wanted to tell Ruby all about. I lean on the door a little and hitch up my bed sheet to stop it from falling. Butler and Gavin would love to haul me in for any infraction, the more embarrassing the better. Indecency fits the bill pretty snug.

My mind races as I play the guessing game. What do they know? Did they find Michelle Wheeler's body? I didn't clean the place up, just got the Hell out of there after Lucifer healed me. My brain had turned to soup. My blood and prints were all over the joint, and trying to explain why I killed her would grant me a one-way ticket to Haven Asylum.

And these goons have been staking me out ever since. *Shit.*

"You know, I get a few inquiries," I mutter, forcing myself to meet their eyes in turn, "but they're pranks, more often than not. They hear about me and spin stories about their great-grandmother haunting a family heirloom they want to sell."

That's happened for real. More than once. Pranks and actual cases.

Lori pushes the door open wider. I slam my hand against it. I haven't extended any invitation and they don't have any legal right to enter.

But I'm starting to panic. Do they know? How? Michelle lived alone, had no family. Dean's gang lost its footing when he died. They'd watch her leave the house, tail her every now and then, but they weren't watching too close considering she managed to build a black altar in her basement. But the PD kept tabs. My sources there said so.

Damn Nick, how sloppy do you wanna get?

"Oh, Nick? You coming back to bed, sugar?"

I spin, and it's a good job the cops can't see my face because I can feel the shock in my expression. A naked leg appears through my bedroom door. Ruby's red-painted toes wiggle, and her head pokes through the gap, a devilish grin on her face and a wicked twinkle in her eye.

"Oh! Excuse me, officers," she gasps in a scandalized voice, though she doesn't withdraw her leg. Instead, an arm comes through, and the door opens a little wider, revealing her bare shoulder and a slither of hip. "Thought maybe the neighbors were giving my young lover a hard time over our... Well, you know..."

I turn back to the cops. The embarrassed smile I'm wearing is 100% genuine.

"Look," I say, half-expecting to see the ghosts of my parents appear behind them, just to make this the most uncomfortable thing that has ever happened to me. "Is this gonna take long? It really is the worst time."

Lori glares over my shoulder at Ruby. Henry's staring daggers at me. "Let's cut the shit, Holleran. You wanna know what we found at your office this morning?"

My shrug is the most indifferent one I can muster, but I'm struggling.

"More like *who* we found," Lori says. I want to scream. "A person of interest. Guy by the name of Marvin Clancy. He's got a reputation for being kind of a freak, like you, See, one freak's all well and good, but when they start hanging out? There's usually trouble. So, how do you know him?"

I shake my head and force the frown forming away from my forehead. "Never said I did."

Henry leans toward me, but I hold my ground. "Yeah, well, he seems to know you. I don't know why he's looking for you, but what you *pretend* to do, it's a fucking scam. Idiots like Marvin Clancy, folks that are sick in the head, they convince themselves that demons roam the streets. Guys like you just make that shit worse. Don't get involved with Clancy or it's going to go badly for you, understand?"

I almost sigh with relief. They don't know about Wheeler, though I need to do something about the place as soon as these bastards leave. What Henry's demanding, I'm more than happy to oblige. I don't want a single thing to do with a Devil Worshipper like Clancy.

And, if he really is a person of interest to them, getting involved will just drag me into their sights. I can't afford to let them subpoena my unabridged case files, the ones I don't send to the PD. It'll hurt a lot of people, Ruby included.

If they think I'm aiding and abetting criminals, it might give them the pretext they need to secure a warrant.

I need to convince Marvin to back off. An idle threat wasn't enough to shake him. That shadow I saw in my office window; I'd bet my bed sheet on it being him. The sonofabitch.

"Fine," I snap, grabbing the door. "Let's say I swing by the precinct in a few days and we can talk it over. Better yet, why don't you call into my office? Monday morning. Is that everything, officers?"

Lori opens her mouth, and I slam the door in her face before she can talk. Damn, that was one of our more courteous visits. They must be starting to like me.

I head back towards the bedroom. Ruby stops me with a hand. "Not so fast, Nick," she laughs, pulling her exposed limbs inside. "You're much too young for me."

"Get dressed," I hiss, just in case the cops have their ears to the door. "We gotta talk."

...

After I've brought her up to speed, Ruby stares at me like I'm the dumbest sack of shit ever to walk the plains of Hell.

"So, you left a place where one of your friends imploded, headed to the home of a *known criminal*—and for the record, everyone knows Wheeler shot you, whether you gave evidence or not—then put a bullet in his wife's head. You left your blood and prints all over their basement, and just went back to your office? What the Hell is wrong with you, Nick?"

Ruby's dressed now. She's sat on the sofa, Diana silent beside her, while I slump in a chair in my bed sheet toga. It's cozy.

"You ever met the Devil before? Kinda leaves an impression, let me tell you. And you know what? Fuck you. A friend of mine died right in front of me and I saw the love of his life watch him ascend to Heaven knowing she couldn't go with him, knowing she was stuck here. Michelle played me good; I'll admit that. Maybe I shoulda taken a step back, assessed things. But I saw her face, Ruby. What Dean Wheeler did to her? That wasn't fake. I couldn't wait to let him finish the job if he turned Aware and Strengthened . I did what I thought was right. What I thought I *had* to do. By the time I realized I'd walked into her trap, it was already too late. And after that? Fuck, I don't even remember arriving back at my office."

Pity flashes in her eyes. Ruby pulls out her cell, types at it a little, then puts it away. It goes without saying she's connected. All kinds frequent The Styx.

"I asked some friends to head over to the Wheelers' and Harry's place. They'll take care of it, but you owe me. Big time. You already did, seeing as I brought you home last night."

"I guess so. And thanks for looking out for the kid."

"Spending time with this young lady is all *my* pleasure, and I'll do it anytime, you hear? I insist."

She takes Diana's hand in hers, and the ghost lays her head on Ruby's shoulder. I understand why the kid feels safe around her. Ruby's a decent soul and grew up with the truth of Hell surrounding her. Not long after she turned six, she died. Choked on a piece of meat, if you can believe it. Her old man brought her back, and she learned Hell the hard way. Sixty years, she lived with the dead around her. Not that you'd think Ruby had seen so many summers by looking at her. Tall, toned, tanned and strong, with her shock of pink hair, Ruby's the picture of health. And, despite being a massive pain in my ass sometimes, she's got the biggest heart.

"I appreciate it, Rubes."

And I do, but business needs attending to and my thoughts have returned to Marvin Clancy, the Devil Worshipper who's decided I'm his personal hook-up to Lucifer himself. At my office, at The Styx. How long before he shows up here? Missing dog, my ass. A pup would run howling from a man like him.

For now, I'm putting a pin in Charon, the mist, and whatever the Hell happened to the Amarok.

"The fella asking for me at the bar last night. You seen him around before?"

"No," she mutters, checking her cell again and stifling a yawn. Ruby's stayed awake all night, I realize. My appreciation deepens. "Who is he?"

"Marvin Clancy. Devil Worshipper."

Ruby bares her teeth. "What did he want? I hope to Christ you're not helping him."

I spread my hands, brows drawing in offence. "Me? Help a Devil Worshipper? Come on, Ruby. He said he could taste the Devil's touch on me, wanted help to summon him."

"And what did you tell him?"

"I told him to fuck off. But he won't give up that easy. Let me know if you see him sniffing around, would you?"

"Sure." Ruby grins. "I'll add it to the list of IOUs. What's your next move with the kid's case?"

I glance at Diana. She's staring through the apartment window at the fading, late-afternoon light, mesmerized by the view my digs boast of city lights and slow-moving traffic.

"Got a couple of leads to follow, but...I've got plans tonight. I'm meeting Rosa for dinner."

Her eyebrows rise. "In the middle of the girl's case?"

"It was her freaking idea!"

Ruby glances at Diana, who offers a sheepish smile and a shrug. She squeezes the girl's hands. The icy touch of the dead doesn't seem to bother her. She shoots me a look, then climbs to her feet. "I guess we all need a little normal, now and then. But you watch your back, Nick."

I watch Ruby leave and turn to see Diana looking my way.

"Can you please get dressed?" she asks, turning back to the window. "I don't know if that's the way people dress at home nowadays, but you're making me uncomfortable."

I nod. Being dead's probably difficult enough without the guy who's supposed to be providing her closure dressed only in a sheet.

"I'll change," I say, climbing to my feet. I grab the TV remote on my way past. "Hey, you like Mickey Mouse?"

Diana nods. Of course. Who doesn't like the Mouse? I flick on a streaming service for the kid to watch while I get to work. There's a few hours left before I meet with Rosa and I mean to put them to use.

Heading to my bedroom, I key my cell, pulling up the number of Zia Bennett, a local reporter I helped a while back on the Whiskey Pete's case. We kept in touch.

Glancing back through the door, I see Diana glued to the screen. The remote is clasped in her colorless hand. She's Strengthening fast. Faster than I thought. I wonder what she's watching. She giggles, other hand covering her mouth as she does. I shake my head. Less than a day in the twenty-first century and she's already binge-watching.

She's still just a kid, despite it all. Out of time, with only me and Ruby to rely on. At least she's not alone.

Zia answers the phone.

"Hey, pal," I say, closing the bedroom door to give me some privacy. "Long time, no see. Wondering if you could help me with some digging."

"Sure thing, Nick. How can I help?"

"It's a strange ask."

"Wouldn't expect anything less from Nick Holleran."

"I'm gonna need records for tenants at the building where my office is for the last...let's say seventy years, with particular attention to 1968. That should cover it."

"Wow, you're right. That is *a strange ask."* I can picture her eager grin, even on the phone. *"You know I'm gonna ask you all about this, next time I see you."*

"I'll give you the exclusive," I reply. "Just let me know what you find. And keep it discreet, yeah?"

"Please. Who do you think you're talking to?"

She hangs up, and my thoughts turn to Rosa. We're meeting tonight and it's hard to focus, but I need to consider the other angles I've got to explore. There's work that needs doing, even though I'm hit with a wave of exhaustion that makes my limbs turn to water. I sink onto my bed, head in my hands, letting the cellphone fall to the mattress.

Truth be told, I need a couple more days rest. My mind's spent. Thoughts come a touch too slow and my reactions feel offbeat. For the briefest moment, I consider bailing on Rosa, but it's a move I've pulled more than I should. This is my chance to make good. It's even more important to make the effort.

Even if I did get fatally stabbed last night. Even if I was saved from death a second time.

I run my hands over my face, raking stubble, then head for the shower.

Can't let Rosa down again. Can't do it to myself either. I'm lucky she even took my calls, responded to my texts.

Tonight's about her. Not the cases, not the ghosts, not me. And I'm *definitely* not going to tell her what she's got in common with the Devil.

ACT NATURALLY

"Sure you don't want me to get you a seat, kid?"

It's funny, but for a ghost with no eyes and crusted blood covering most of her face, I'm getting real good at reading Diana's expressions. The one she's wearing now tells me she thinks I'm dumb as all shit.

"I've been standing for sixty years, Nick. Another hour won't hurt. Especially because I don't feel pain. Besides, might look weird having three chairs at a romantic dinner for two."

She finishes by sticking her tongue out.

The kid's got a point. Rosa knows how this world works—I told her a long time ago, about Hell and the ghosts, and she took it like the champ she is—but for everyone else? Yeah, weird.

Plus, Rosa told me no ghost talk for one night. Having a dead girl sitting at the table with us might kill the mood. I aim to hold up my side of the bargain.

"You're nervous," Diana says.

"No shit," I mutter, then grimace. Shouldn't swear in front of the kid.

"Just relax, Nick."

"Starting to wish I'd left you at home."

"Why didn't you? I wanted to find out if Moana managed to return the Heart of Te Fiti."

"Because you came Aware the night after Lucifer brought me back from the brink. A few hours later, I run into Charon, an Amarok, a Devil Worshipper and whatever the Hell was in that mist. I'm not letting you out of my sight."

Diana's lips twitch, annoyed, so I throw her a smile.

"Besides, I need you here. Smartest decision I made was listening to you when you told me to do this tonight. And I need all the help I can get."

I pause as a server moves by. Don't want people to think I'm talking to myself. Happens more often than I'd like, truth be told.

I'm being honest with her. Fighting demons, expunging ghosts, these are things I understand. Dating, not so much. Tonight's important—for me, for Rosa—and I'm running on empty. Energy drinks will only take me so far. I need a real friend. One that doesn't turn my guts to rot. I'm going to push myself for this. If the Wheeler case taught me anything, it's that I have to live my life.

I've acted like a schmuck with Rosa too many times, and I'm not about to repeat my mistakes if I can help it.

"I've blown it so many times with Rosa. Too fu— Too stubborn. Too much baggage, but she keeps giving me chances, you know? More than she should. All I do to repay her is let her down. I shoulda died the other night—again—but I'm gonna do better. Look forward. I'm living for a reason, and Rosa's part of that. If she'd turned right that night when

I was bleeding out in that alleyway…"

"You held that against her," Diana says. She doesn't need empathy to figure that out.

Yeah, I did hold it against her. And then, at the Wheelers' place, I cost myself my own place in Heaven. Rosa didn't do that. *I* did. It's time to stop blaming her.

Instead, I glance around Tony's and admire Rosa's choice of restaurant. It's busy. Swanky in a relaxed, low-key kind of way. The guys are all in shirtsleeves and slacks, the girls in fitted dresses or pantsuits. A pianist taps out some light jazz in the corner and, somehow, it's almost ghost free, Diana aside.

You go anywhere in Haven city, you'll see the dead. It's just the way things are. Tony's ain't no exception, but the ones here fade into the background. There's nothing horrific about them; there's no pain. Most of them are Aware, but they're taking in the sights, enjoying the music, living vicariously through the alive. It's not the worst place to haunt.

Old Tony himself lingers here, ten years dead, sitting in an armchair in the corner that no one else dares to use, watching his empire persist. He used to be part of the Family. Mafioso. He ended up the way most of those types do—filled with lead. Of course, Tony had a place in Hell. They run a tight ship, like they know the boss is still watching, and the food's delicious.

"Almost 8pm," Diana says, nodding towards the massive, art deco clock on the wall. A small part of my brain asks how she sees.

It ain't all that important, Nick.

"Did you always state the obvious, or is that how you're

Strengthening?" I ask. If in doubt, rely on smart-ass quips.

Diana sniffs, but her lips curl into a faint smile. "Momma always said I was a know-it-all."

"You were the oldest. You had to be."

I pull out my cell and bring up the camera, baring my teeth at it. I've checked they're clean too many times already, but what's the harm in one more? Not that I'll admit it, but I made an effort tonight; my thick, blonde hair's combed and styled to the side, and I shaved the scruff from my cheeks. Even wore my best black shirt, jacket and pants combo. No sneakers, either. Fine boots tonight.

Diana sniggered when I emerged from my bedroom, asked me if I knew Johnny Cash. On the way to the restaurant, she asked if Charon had left too much of an impression on me. All I needed was the cloak.

I'm starting to like the kid.

"Nick?"

Diana points at the window. My heart thuds and my stomach lurches, but it ain't Rosa. No. Kid's gesturing outside, to a thin mist oozing across the street, tendrils curling against the wide windows. Just like the fog in Meadow Park.

"Coincidence?" I ask, but I already know the answer.

Diana shakes her head. "I feel them out there. That rage. That fear. That hunger. It's the same as the park. Do you think it's Charon?"

"No," I mutter. "Charon doesn't have friends. He doesn't travel with an entourage. I reckon he just picked his moment to appear. Maybe he thought he'd see 'the Fateless' meet his end. I've run into Charon before, and that mist, that smell... Well, I've never seen it before."

"Should we leave?"

I hesitate. I chew my lip, lean my elbows on the table so I can think straight. We took a cab over here. Now I wish I'd brought the Mustang. I'd be happier to have a quick getaway if something's hunting us. I'm carrying my Ruger, but that's all. Bullets ain't even doused in holy water. Rookie mistake, but I've not had the chance to take stock of my supplies. Guess I relied on Harry and Maeve too much in keeping me prepared for Hell. I'm vulnerable without them in so many ways.

I frown at the table, as if the tasteful silk cloth will reveal a way out to me. Those creatures in the mist, they want us alone. We escaped Meadow Park, and they didn't follow. God knows where the fucking Amarok ended up. Logic says it's safer to stay at Tony's, at least for now. Though me and logic don't often see eye-to-eye.

I open my mouth to tell Diana the plan.

"Half-expected to find an empty table waiting for me. You scrub up good, Nick."

My elbow slips, bouncing my chin off the edge of the table. I scramble to my feet, shrugging it off, pretending it never happened. I plaster the lopsided, disarming smile onto my face.

It's her.

Rosa Riberio—Head Tech at the Library of Haven City and the woman who brought me back from death—smiles at me. Laughter dances in her eyes. Too many months have passed since I saw her last. She's wearing her wavy, dark hair loose over the shoulder of her red-and-blue plaid shirt. Her hands are in the pockets of her jeans, though she's wearing heels so she's almost the same height as me. It's been too long...

Something wells in my chest. This warm, fuzzy thing that makes my eyes water, just a little.

Happiness? Well, sonofabitch. The smile plastered on my old face ain't fake.

"You gonna say anything, Nick?" Diana whispers. Not sure why; Rosa won't hear her. "Or you just gonna stare at her all night?"

I cough. "Hey, I try. Thought I'd get here early for once. Make a good first impression."

"First?" Rosa raises her eyebrows. "We're a ways past first impressions at this point, Nick."

"Pull out her chair," Diana hisses.

I throw her a look—*butt outta this*—but I do as she says. Manners don't cost a dime, after all. Rosa sits down with a laugh, her eyes wide in sham surprise. At least, I think she's mocking me. She smiles at a passing waiter, and orders a bottle of red wine. It sounds expensive.

"You're paying, remember?" Rosa says, with a wink.

"Is that what I said?" I shrug. "Can't remember. Maybe I'm getting old."

"You wouldn't be planning to renege on your promise of a free meal, would you?"

"Ain't the pleasure of my company enough for you?"

Rosa shrugs and turns to her menu, though she's still smiling when she glances up at me.

"So, Nick Holleran," she says, glancing around. "How many unseen friends do we have with us tonight?"

I catch Diana in the corner of my eye. Her head's

tilting back and forth between us, like she's watching a tennis match. I pour a little water into my glass and let out a long-suffering sigh.

"Thought you said no ghost talk tonight."

"There's *always* going to be ghosts, Nick. There's always going to be cases. Did you think I expected that to all disappear? I'm here, aren't I? I know what I'm getting into."

She doesn't. Things have escalated since we were last together. And maybe there will always be ghosts, but there don't have to be tonight.

"Actually, things are pretty quiet. I guess Tony's is just for the living."

Diana sighs rolls her eyes—at least, I think she does—but I ignore her. I'm lying, yes, but Rosa deserves better than to be surrounded by the dead without ever knowing it. I turned her world upside down when I told her about Hell, whether she admits it or not. Tonight is the start of something different and I'm going to do a better job protecting her this time.

She reaches out, takes my hand and squeezes it. "I'm sorry about Harry and Maeve. I know what they meant to you. How have you been? It must still be pretty raw, right?"

I stare at our hands, clasped together, and squeeze back.

"Guess it ain't sunk in yet," I reply, before staring into those dark eyes of hers and smiling. "But...we don't need to talk about it tonight. They'd want me to try and act natural and normal. Lord knows they told me often enough. Truth's a gift, not a burden. I want to know about you. How've *you* been?"

Rosa squeezes my hand once more, then lets go. The warmth of her hand ebbs away, leaving my palm cool and uncomfortable.

"I'll tell you all about it," she says, getting to her feet, "but first, I gotta pee!"

With a laugh, she heads to the restroom. I feel Diana watching me.

"How am I doing, kid?"

"She likes you. But she's frustrated. She wants this to work, but she's afraid of what might happen."

Frustration. Makes sense. I've shut myself away from her too much in the past. Every time we grow close, I pull away. I've tried being open with her, but it's instinct to curl up tight, and I'm terrible at explaining that to her.

Last time we spoke, Rosa told me I had a fear of commitment and maybe she's right, to a degree. But it's not just that. Like the kid said earlier, Rosa saved me, but in doing so, she opened my eyes to Hell and kept me from Heaven. I had trouble unpacking all that, but I won't use it as an excuse any longer, even if I have to rewire my brain to make it work.

Still, the kid's report is promising.

"She *just* likes me?" I ask Diana, falling silent when the waiter brings our wine over.

"That's not for me to say. But you're lucky she stuck around for you. She's nice."

I watch the waiter pour and find it hard to disagree. Through the restaurant's windows, the mist thickens, swirls and presses up against the window. No one else notices.

I'll do my best to blend in with the folk enjoying their time in Hell, if only for an hour or so.

...

"Wait, wait, wait. You've got a *boyfriend*?"

The steak—rare, almost blue—hovers near my lips, skewered on the end of my fork. Here's me thinking I'm succeeding at a first date, and Rosa drops this bombshell in the middle of the main course.

"Had," Rosa clarifies, and I stick the meat in my mouth to hide the grin attempting to bloom on my face. I chew to keep my jaw busy. "What? You think just because Nick Holleran isn't in the picture I'm sitting at home, leaping at my cell every time it vibrates, hoping it's the mysterious Paranormal Investigator? I thought you knew me better than that, Nick."

A trap. I glance at Diana, and she's fixed on me with that stare of hers. Fifteen, but she knows one wrong syllable from me could spell catastrophe. So I bide my time. Grabbing the bottle of red—did I mention how expensive it is?—I refill her glass. Mine too. I even give my wrist a little twist at the end, making the rim neat, all professional-like. I catch Rosa's eye and the grin makes its triumphant appearance.

"Don't give me that look, Holleran." She says it a little pouty, but her smile's twinkling at me. "Still think you're a charmer, huh?"

I shrug and spread my hands. "Hey, I'm just trying to be honest. And the fact is, you were never really one to pine. If I'm acting like a schmuck, why wouldn't you live your life? No matter what happens, I know we'd still be friends. Eventually."

Rosa considers me. I gulp down my steak and my ego.

"It's hard, dating people who don't know how the world really works, y'know?" she says, mimicking my voice. Yeah, I said that once or twice. A good excuse for acting like an ass.

"Not really. Only girl I dated, I told the truth. Figured I owed her that much for taking a chance on me."

In the corner of my vision, Diana sighs and nods. Gotta admit, the kid's real helpful.

Rosa leans her cheek into a fist and taps one finger on the table, frowning at me, like I'm a puzzle she hasn't figured out how to solve yet. It's just a matter of time.

"Who's helping you?"

Shit.

I can only blink and give my head a confused wobble as my mind goes into a blind panic. I don't even wanna look in Diana's direction.

I rub at the back of my neck. "Well…"

"Let me guess. Some kind of fairy, right? A nymph? Or, like, a vampire maybe?" Rosa considers, then shakes her head. "No. Too toxic, right? Maybe you just started listening when Ruby speaks for a change."

I hold my hands up. "You got me."

"Hmm…" Rosa contemplates her nails. "My compliments to your instructor. I'd give this date a solid eight out of ten so far."

I lean forward. "So, what did I lose points on?"

Rosa smiles, arches an eyebrow. Man, do I want to kiss her. "You want your feedback now? We're not even at dessert yet. Sure you don't want to try a little bit harder to see if you can make a perfect score?"

I join in with her laughter.

"How's work?" I ask.

She used to hate how I never asked her about that. I didn't do it out of spite or anything; I just forget to ask people. Maybe because I spend so much time dodging those kinds of questions myself.

Rosa's eyes go wide, and she takes a sip of her wine. "Oh, you know, busy. Getting a lot of people coming in with flyers lately, pets going missing. You heard about that?"

"Yeah," I reply, thinking of the posters behind the bar in The Styx. "Seen them about."

"Weird, huh?"

The nerves I had melted away as soon as we polished off the first bottle of red, and me and Rosa got to yapping like no time had passed at all. With a little help from the kid, I steer the conversation away from ghosts and demons and my encounter with Michelle Wheeler. It's difficult, because Rosa *wants* to know. She wants to be a part of it all. I'll ease her into it. Just not tonight.

After two hours, and another bottle, I decide to throw caution to the goddamn wind.

"Rosa, I missed you."

Silence. I take a quick glance at Diana, who's so embarrassed she's turned around and staring through Tony's windows. Rosa just peers over her wine glass at me, and I wish I really had taken some advice from Ruby.

"Sorry, that's not fair. Got no damned right to say that, all the times I've messed you around. Screwed things up."

A touch on the forearm shakes me from my cringing. Rosa's hand lies on my shirt cuff.

"You're being honest with me. You know I prefer that." She pulls away. "Since we're being honest, I missed you too. But how's this time going to be different from all the other times, huh? We can drink wine in a fancy restaurant, but what about tomorrow? Are you going to let me help? Are you going to let me *in*? You've pushed me away so many times."

"Too many times?"

Rosa meets my eyes, breath caught somewhere between her lungs and my heart. "I don't know."

I can only nod. Look, maybe she shouldn't give me another chance. We never fought, never screamed at one another. But she always said she could see me turning into a ghost, growing more distant, just when our relationship was getting serious. It's like we were hiking a mountain together, and each time we neared the top, I'd quit on her. I'd let work pile up, tell her I was busy, cancel dates, stop taking calls. And then there was the way we met.

I brought that up a lot, used it as a barrier to stop us growing closer. You can only do that to a person so much before something's gotta give, right?

"I mean, I wouldn't say no to doing this again. And soon," Rosa murmurs, signaling a waiter, "but make me a promise, Nick."

"What?"

"Don't mess me around again. If you get cold feet, I don't want any games. Just tell me straight." I open my mouth to reply, but she cuts me off. "And don't tell me you ain't gonna mess me around. No empty promises. Just actions, Nick. Prove it to me. Deal?"

I give her the old, lopsided grin. "You wanna shake on it?"

"Smart ass."

It's bold, but I take her hand. Hold it for a second, feel the warmth of it, the smoothness against my rough fingers, and meet her eyes. "I get it, and I'm serious. If I let you down this time, don't answer my calls again, don't give me another chance. I won't deserve it. Hell, reckon I don't really deserve this one."

"You're trying," Rosa smiles, squeezing my fingers and easing her hand free. "And I want this if *you* want it, so let's give it a shot, okay?"

We fall into a peaceful silence as Rosa waits for the waiter so she can order dessert. I guess she'll order the chocolate fudge cake, and she does. With two spoons.

"Nick!"

I turn so fast in Diana's direction that it looks weird, so I start coughing. Mist's so thick outside that it's pressed against the pane, a grey curtain blocking off the outside world but that's not what the kid's pointing at. By the window, lowering himself into a chair, is Marvin goddamn Clancy. He nods and gives me a small salute. The fog gathers against the window behind him like a cloak.

I feel my teeth grind. That sonofabitch. I warned him to stay away. He's tailing me. For certain, he is. Naw, that ain't happening.

I turn to Rosa. "Okay, in the interest of our new arrangement, I'm gonna tell you this straight..." I keep my voice light and low, like I'm about to whisper up some sweet nothings. She gives me a sharp look, anyway. "Don't stare at him, but there's a heavy-set guy sat by the window looking our way. You see him?"

Rosa dabs at her mouth with a napkin, flutters her eyes. I see `em dart in Marv's direction before she gives me the slightest of nods. She's good.

"Punk's stuck to me like my shadow. His name's Marvin Clancy and he's bad news. I don't want him causing trouble. Not for you, or anyone else here. I'm gonna head to the little boys' room, and I'm guessing old Marv's gonna follow. Me and him will have a quick chat, and he's gonna leave, all in time for dessert."

Rosa chews her lips, pensive. "Nick, is he an ordinary case or...a special one?"

"He's not so special," I say, and I'm not lying. Devil Worshippers like him are a dime a dozen.

She lets out a relieved sigh. "Y'know, just when I thought me and Nick Holleran could have a normal date like regular people, you get a tail. Okay, fine, but make it quick, or I'm compensating myself with your half of the cake."

I could kiss her, but Marv's watching and so's the kid. She might not take it well anyway. It's been awhile since we had that kind of access to each other and we need to work back to it, I know. I wink instead, and get to work.

I'm carrying my Ruger, so I didn't take my jacket off. My fingers rest on the grip as I head to the restroom. I see Marv following me as I glance in a mirror outside.

Nice.

Pushing my way into the restroom, I form a quick plan. I've got seconds.

"Anyone in here?"

No answer. Excellent.

I'm handy, but Marv's a giant. The Devil-worshipping creep could toss me around like a rubber ball before I could land a punch. So I need an edge. Opposite the restroom door is a stall, unoccupied. I slide against the wall and draw the Ruger.

Marv pushes his way in. In one movement, I grab his arm and pull. He loses his balance through sheer surprise. The door slams shut behind him. I hammer the barrel of my Ruger against the back of his neck. Marv grunts, still falling forwards. Now, I'm steering him, head first into the door of the stall.

The frame shakes as he collides with it. He falls, catching his forehead on the ceramic bowl. I follow him in, kicking the door shut behind me and locking it, before putting my whole weight on Marv's back, pinning him to the floor as I straddle him, trapping his arms with my knees. I jam the business end of my Ruger against his cheek.

Cozy.

"Thought I told you to stay away, Marv." I flick the safety off the Ruger. "Caught you lurking around my office—twice—and now you're following me here? Seems like we're gonna have a problem. Are we?"

Marv hasn't said a word since his collision with the stall door, but he's breathing. Big, wet, ragged lungfuls of air. Now he's wheezing, and it takes me a moment to realize the crazy bastard's laughing.

"If you won't help me, Mr. Holleran, I'll take what I need."

I press the Ruger harder against his face. It just makes him laugh more. "What the Hell d'ya mean by that, huh?"

"I saw the Nephilim watching you. Talking to you. I'm willing to wager the Devil wouldn't want to see you harmed, Mr. Holleran. Why go to all the trouble otherwise?" The sonofabitch places the flats of his hands against the floor and pushes, teeth gritted, and fuck me if he doesn't lift me off the ground. I smack him on the head again, not hard enough to cause real damage, but enough to get his attention. He quakes with laughter. "You caught me by surprise tonight, Mr. Holleran. Perhaps I underestimated you. I will not make the same mistake again."

I stick the Ruger in his ear.

"I see you again, Marv, I won't need to surprise you."

Marv's stalked me halfway across Haven and now he's crashed my date and threatened my life. If he comes after me again, even Butler and Gavin would be hard-pressed to say I wasn't justified in putting him down.

"And don't forget, your ghost won't be safe from me either. I want you out of this restaurant, right now, or I'm calling the cops. Sounds like they've got an interest in you."

"Everyone is interested in something, Mr. Holleran."

Snarling, I lift the Ruger, about to hit the sorry sack of shit again. The opening of the restroom door stops me.

"Last chance," I hiss, climbing off him and unlocking the door. "I'm warning you."

Marv chuckles, turning his head so he can see me. His face is a mess. A ragged cut oozes blood down one side of his face, staining his teeth as he leers at me.

"Be seeing you, Mr. Holleran."

I back out of the stall, Ruger trained on him but hidden by the door. Diana stands just inside the restroom, hands on hips, pits fixed on me. Wonder if anyone saw the door open and close all by itself?

Like I said before, ghosts can interact with things in Hell; chairs, glasses, the living. They don't have to touch things either. Some can use their minds—people call `em poltergeists in the movies and whatnot—but they gotta focus. The force she exerted on that door, Diana must have put some serious effort into it.

"Come on," I say, jamming the Ruger into its holster. "Don't want anyone seeing me leaving, especially if they get a look at Marv's mug."

"Nick," she hisses, voice thick with rising panic, "the mist's getting worse. I can hear them, howling, snarling. We can't go outside."

Shit.

"I'll handle it," I whisper.

I head back to Rosa. She smiles as I sit down and points to the half-eaten chocolate fudge cake with its melted vanilla ice cream topping. I smooth down my hair, jostled by my altercation with Marv, and adjust my jacket. My heart's thumping something rotten, like a hare banging his old bunny feet against the ground.

"Saved you some. I must like you more than I thought."

"You finish it," I say, glancing around for a waiter. "I know it's your favorite."

"Nick Holleran," Rosa grins, "you never fail to amaze. Everything okay with your stalker?"

Marv strolls by as I'm picking up the check and asking

the waiter to call us a cab. He meets my eyes, and his black, shark-like orbs glitter with malice. A wad of paper pressed against his forehead, blood on his collar. There's no smile this time, no look of adulation. Marvin Clancy flat-out hates my guts. I watch him till he leaves Tony's and merges with the thick mist.

"I took care of it. Pretty sure he got the message." A thought occurs to me as we leave our table. "Say, you still doing Aikido?"

I'm pretty confident with the Ruger and my fists and feet, but I'd feel better knowing Rosa's still a practicing martial artist. We're about to head out on the street and there's a Devil Worshipper on the loose, and Lord only knows what else.

"Nick, I *teach* Aikido now. So, this guy got the message, but he's not going to back off, is he?"

"He will. I was just wondering, is all."

She raises an eyebrow. There's no fooling this woman. "Come on, Nick. Don't start jerking me around now. You only just started being straight with me. You're worried about this guy, right?"

"Look, I told him next time I lay eyes on him, I'll call the cops. They're interested in him, anyway." She gives me that look again, makes me raise my palms, all defensive-like. "Rosa, I promise. Got the PD on speed-dial. I so much as smell him, that's what I'll do."

She nods. "Okay. I'm going to believe you on this, Nick. Maybe I had too much wine, huh?"

We make small talk in the lobby and I try to appear engaged, switched-on and not as fucking anxious as I am.

Rosa collects her jacket when the cab arrives. Diana's stuck to my side like a shiver as we head out onto the sidewalk. I can't see shit in all this fog, though Rosa doesn't notice it at all. I feel a weight on me again. Something's watching, out there in the mist. Beyond it, I hear the snuffling, the growling. The stench of rot.

Flesh... Fresh blood... Sweet, sweet meat... It calls to us... So hungry... It gnaws... Stop the pain... Feed us... Free us...

I open the cab door. Diana flows into it, her face pressed up against the window on the far side as she peers into the thick, grey gloom.

"I'm not going home with you, Nick," Rosa says, thumping me on the arm.

It almost makes me draw my Ruger. Shit, my nerves! That...presence. What is it?

"Ah, no, of course not," I stutter. Rosa laughs. Reckon she thinks she's caught me in some caddish ploy. "Give you a ride?"

"Nah, I'll get my own. You've given me a lot to think about tonight. But you should go home and get your beauty sleep, okay?"

She presses her hands to my chest, like she did five years ago when she held the blood inside my body. This time, it's gentle. A caress. Rosa reaches up and presses her lips on mine. For a moment, I forget about the mist, Marvin Clancy and whatever else lurks out there.

Just for a moment.

"I'll see you in the week?" Rosa asks, as she pulls away.

"Sure," I say, catching her fingers with mine as she lets her hand drop from my chest. "Anytime."

Rosa laughs. "I'll call you."

"Hey, you know what? Why don't you take my cab?" I smile, trying to stop my eyeballs from darting around. "I'll pay. Least I can do if I can't take you home myself."

"You sure?"

"I'll get the next one."

"Why, Nick. Such a gentleman" Rosa laughs as she hops into the back seat without a worry. Jamming my hands in my pockets, I pull out a handful of notes and toss them to the driver. "Anywhere she wants to go, buddy."

The lights of the cab merging with the mist mesmerizes me as it pulls away, until a piercing howl sends me slamming back into the wall of the restaurant beside Diana. She clings to me, and I ignore her biting cold as it floods across my body.

Another cab drifts past, cutting through the fog. I whistle my damned loudest and my sudden good fortune holds out when its tires screech.

"Where to, Nick?" Diana asks, her voice high-pitched and so childlike.

I rack my brains. Marvin Clancy's watching me. He knows where I work, maybe found where I live. Can't go to The Styx, either. The Devil Worshipper and the cops are both watching my regular haunts. Somewhere unexpected then, far away from here.

"You know Redwood and Maine?" I ask the cab driver. He nods into his rearview. "Take me there on a long, winding route, pal."

Diana grows still next to me. Redwood and Maine. That's where she used to live. The kid hired me to do a job, and if I can't go home or back to my office, then I may as well get started. It's somewhere Marvin Clancy and whatever's hunting me won't think of. I just hope to Him upstairs this mist doesn't follow us there too.

As the cab pulls away from the sidewalk and into its lane, I stare out the window. A face appears in the fog.

Marvin Clancy's.

The freak's eyes lock with mine, and this time, he grins, his crimson teeth shining through the murk. The cab leaves him behind, and the howls and screams in the mist dim as we head to Diana's old home. She takes my hand, grips it tight.

"This okay, kid?" I whisper. "Redwood and Maine. Couldn't think of anywhere else."

"Yes," she nods. "No time like the present."

She falls silent, but she doesn't let go. Not that I blame her. She's just a kid, and in my experience, going home's never fun.

TWO OF US

"Why're you stopping, pal?"

The frown forms when the cab comes to an abrupt halt. We left the mist behind miles back. It took us a while, but now we're in a part of Haven I've never seen before. Outside, washed-out ghosts loiter. Lots of `em, but not much else—no buildings, no cars, no nothing. My hackles, which only just settled down, think it's party time again.

"Redwood and Maine," the driver drawls. He taps his GPS to prove it. "You getting out or just sightseeing? It's forty-four dollars either way."

Diana's got her face pressed to the window, hands flat against the glass. Her back's to me, but I recognize the tension. This ain't right.

"Not staying long," I say. "Leave the meter running, yeah?"

"You're the boss, man."

Stepping out of the car, a biting chill sinks its teeth into me. Weather's gone to shit in Hell of late, but I'm not sure if the temperature plummeted or my body's trying to tell me something. Full moon's hanging in the sky and stars are piercing the velvet night. The sight should set anyone at ease. Not me.

Redwood and Maine's a wasteland. If anyone lived here, decades have gone by since. And the ghosts... It's not often I see so many in one place. Must be about thirty of them, none of them Aware. Diana's fingers lock with mine again. I'm getting used to the sensation when she does it.

"Kid, something bad happened here."

So I'm Detective Obvious again, but I gots to say something.

"I can feel it. So much grief and fear. It's everywhere, and it's so hot."

Hot? Now she says it, I can almost feel the lick of flames warming me, but it's distant. The grey form of a ghost wanders by, and on instinct, I turn Diana's face away so she doesn't have to look at what I see.

He's a boy, a teenager, just like her. I can tell he's black from the skin on his forearms, but if he wore a sweater instead of a plain white tee, I wouldn't know it. His face is a mess. Skin's melted right off and one eyeball's missing too, though I reckon the heat popped it before he died.

This kid burned to death in a fire.

He screams, and Diana drops into a ball, covering her ears. I want to do the same, but I'm transfixed by the boy. He's howling, and there's so much goddamn pain as his skinny arms wrap around his body. It doesn't last long. He flickers and disappears. Caught in a loop, doomed to exist this way for all time. The boy's screams echo in my mind.

"How could you fucking do this?" I mutter, staring up at the Heavens. I hope the Big Guy up there's listening. "What could a kid do to deserve this fate for eternity, you sonofabitch?"

Across the sidewalk, I see the boy reappear and begin making his way over.

"Diana..." I kneel so I'm face-to-face with her. "We can go. We don't have to stay here. I can do some digging, find out what happened, and I can come back another time, alone. But we should go. That kid's coming back and I ain't gonna let you hear that again."

I don't realize how much I mean that until I say it. The kid's seen enough. She's been through...Hell.

"It's so much! The screams, Nick! I can hear the flames popping, surrounding me, hot fingers clutching at me. There's so much death. But... I can't go. Nick, I need to know. Momma, my sisters. I have to find out. Please, help me through this."

I take her hand again and pull her close.

"Let's do it then, but stay close. And if I say look away, do it."

We pass the burning boy and I follow my own advice, keep my stare fixed ahead. Other ghosts are milling around, all locked in this nightmare. Men, women and children of all ages congregate across the street on a concrete clearing, where the intersection meets.

"There," Diana says, pointing ahead. "That's where our tenement used to be. Took up this whole block."

Makes sense. Most of the ghosts are crowding where the kid says, like they died inside their apartments. But something leveled the place. If a fire broke out, turned the joint to rubble, no one bothered to rebuild it. They swept it clear and forgot about it.

Until yesterday, I hadn't heard of Redwood and Maine

in Haven, though we're so far out I'm not sure we're even in the city. This place was a dirty secret, scrubbed from the face of Hell. Bile floods my gullet.

"Fire! Fire! Please, help! Save my babies!"

I freeze and close my eyes. Diana stops too. Breathing in deep, I crack an eye open, hoping to Christ above the woman screaming for her life ain't the kid's mom. I know Diana's family are dead, and I reckon she does too, but I don't want her seeing it. I don't want them trapped in Hell for God's fickle reasons.

The woman's hovering above us, on an upper floor that no longer exists, like she's yelling through a window out at the street.

"Kid..."

She cuts me off. "No."

I let out the breath caught in my chest. Still, I watch the woman. Watch her burn. She's still screaming for help, but a deep agony and panic fills her cries. She yells two words. "My babies!" That's it. Over and over, until it hits me. Folk must have stood on the sidewalk, watching the whole place raze to the ground.

"What the fuck happened here?" I ask no one in particular.

Diana shrugs away from my hand and moves amongst the other ghosts. I should stop her, but I don't. She needs this. I realize she might know some of these folk. From the way they're dressed, I'd put my Mustang on this fire happening in the 60s. Must have been after Diana died, since she thought this place was still here.

Related? I'm believing less in coincidence.

"Fateless."

I shoulda expected Charon to show up. I didn't feel that presence watching me again, the one that's dogged my steps since I left my office with Diana last night. Guess I can rule out the Ferryman as the cause. Even so, my anger just needed a spark. And Charon, that bastard, has provided it.

"You escaped with your life again, I see. I thought the Amarok or the mist might bring you into my arms, but not to be. This time."

I spin, grab the smug sonofabitch by his lapels and pull him so close his Clint Eastwood-looking face is almost touching mine. I force myself to meet his eyes and what I see there...it knocks the anger out of me.

Centuries—no, eons—of cold disregard peer back at me. Those eyes, they don't see the way ours do. He's not a demon, but I'm not sure what he is. There's humanity buried in there—ancient, almost forgotten—and a dull, faded color now turned to grey, like someone tried to affect some semblance of humanity. But there's a void of conscience, of feeling.

There isn't a soul hiding behind those eyes. Not one someone like me can comprehend anyway.

"All these people, Charon. Dead, and for what?" I'm pleading, like I need a reason—any goddamned reason—for all this. "You just let `em linger here? Children, you bastard. This is all they've got? To die over and over again?"

Charon shrugs. "That is their lot, Fateless. I do not make the rules. I ensure the balance, until it is no longer required."

Balance? The Ferryman takes a step back, and the darkness that follows him swells.

"Can't you do something?" I growl. "I thought all children were innocent?"

"That is what your priests tell you to give you comfort. Ironic, given that many of them are sinners themselves. In God's eyes, all that live have sinned. They must prove their innocence through life."

"Not all kids, or Hell would overflow with them."

"You think you understand how Hell works? Such arrogance. But no, children are taught innocence. Some lose it with haste." Charon points towards the boy with the melted face, screaming near the cab and its oblivious driver. "He stole a toy from a neighbor. A spinning top. A trivial item, but the sin was there. Greed. Envy. Vanity in believing he deserved where others did not."

"Why follow that fickle sonofabitch upstairs? You don't have to follow his rules. Not for something like this."

Charon stares at me, and his expression is almost reproachful. I pull out a cigarette and get to lighting it, trying to keep the tremble out of my hands.

"What? I can say what I like about Him. I committed revenge, remember? I ain't getting into Heaven."

Charon points over my shoulder.

"She stole food. More than once. Money from the cash register where she worked went into her pockets."

I glance over and see Diana, standing near a boy her age. "Diana?"

"Your ward, yes. She has no passage into Heaven."

Even though I've taken one drag, I throw the cigarette to the floor and stamp on it, taking out my frustrations in the only way I can.

"She did that to feed her family. Would He have been

happier if she'd let them starve? Isn't it a sin not to do your duty by your kin?"

"*Stealing* is a sin," Charon replies, without missing a beat. His voice is like a shovel scraping through loose stones.

"So, you're telling me after she meets her purpose, she's stuck here? Forever?"

"Nothing is forever, Fateless, and some do not receive the pleasure of turning their faces towards the sky."

What the Hell is he even talking about?

"Nick!"

I glance around as Diana calls. She's waving me over, and the boy she's talking to stares my way.

"Fateless," Charon whispers, laying a bony hand with only a slither of flesh on my shoulder. I go numb, like that side of my body ceases to exist. "If it is of any comfort, her family are in Heaven."

"Maybe it will be," I bite out. "But she won't see `em again. How's that fair?"

I stride away, sensation returning as I shake off Charon's touch. Felt like half my body had fallen into the grave.

I approach the kids. The boy Diana's talking to blinks at me, a confused look washing across his face, followed by a blank one. He's cycling, features slack, then surprised. He's half-Aware, like his memories are coming back. Diana clutches his hand.

The little boy's five. Maybe six. Small, nothing but skin and bone when he lived. His eyes are huge, standing out on his gaunt, innocent face. Fuck this. Fuck it all.

Diana's jaw, below the crusted blood on her cheeks, is tight. She's holding herself together. One tough cookie. Not sure I could do the same in her position. Almost can't now.

If the boy she's talking to ate more than one hot meal a week, I'm a saint. The kid suffered in life. Now he's doing the same in death. Where's the justice in any of this?

"Nick, this is Louis. I knew him. Louis, tell my friend what you told me."

The boy squints up at me, so I crouch and give him a smile.

"It's okay, kid. You can talk to me." That unseen weight presses on me again. I glance over my shoulder. Charon's gone, but out there, in the darkness of Redwood and Maine, something's watching me. Again.

No mist this time. No screams, other than those of the dead, dying all over again.

"They came," Louis says, before falling silent again. Diana's looking the other way, but still holding his hand. He looks around, cowers a little, then furrows his brow. "White men came. They were saying we forgot our place, said they'd teach us a lesson. I heard Diana's momma screaming, yelling at them about taking her girl. She said she'd gone to the police. That's when the fire started. That's..."

Louis pauses, his face slack. I grip his thin shoulder.

"Go on, kid. Hey! Stick with me."

He sighs. "Her mom said a white man took her girl. They came during the night, a mob. They...they started it. The fire. I can still hear them laughing. They said they'd teach us all a lesson about respecting our betters."

Diana lets go of Louis' hand, and he cowers on the floor, hands over his head, peering up above him. He screams and falls flat, as if the rafters just collapsed on him.

I pull Diana close. She's shaking with sobs. I stoop, lift her up and head back to the cab, ignoring the presence watching me, questions turning over in my mind.

Diana got a kid stuck in a loop to communicate. How'd she do that? The Empathy? Smells like more than that.

And what Charon said... It's clear I ain't got Hell figured out yet.

If I don't figure some of this out soon, the two of us are in real trouble.

...

The cops, Marvin and the mist are out there, tailing me, and that's assuming my old friend, the Amarok, ain't still on my trail too. We take the cab to a motel on the outskirts of Haven instead. 'The Ace in the Hole'. I tip the driver and advise he forgets all about us. The guy in reception gives me a funny look when I ask for twin beds, but I reckon he's had stranger requests.

Diana sits on the edge of her single as I scroll through my cell, looking through articles sent by Zia about Redwood and Maine. I asked her to see what she could find when we left the vacant lot and she worked fast.

The place burned down alright. At the time, the investigators filed it as an accident. In the late-90s, the case was reopened and reclassified as racially-motivated felony murder. The press wasn't interested in an almost 30-year-old cold case, though more likely too many of the people involved held positions of power, or were related to those who do.

Louis' story checks out. A lynch mob came for the

woman accusing a white man of taking her girl. Things got ugly when the folk in the building didn't hand her over.

Diana stayed silent for the entire cab ride. Then, when we got to the room, she asked me what Charon and I talked about. Taking a lesson from my date with Rosa, I told her the truth.

Look, I know she's a child, but she deserves to know what happened to her family.

She only said four words. "I'm happy they're together."

What can you say to that?

"We used to have a record player," Diana says. It's good to hear her talking so I just keep my trap shut and listen. "Daddy brought it home one night. We set it up by the window, even though we didn't have much of a view. Momma would sing, the girls would dance. It seems like yesterday, but... So many years have gone by, haven't they?"

A question to no one. Coming to terms with Hell is tough. I know from experience, and, in all honesty, I don't think I'm quite there yet. Can't imagine how a kid deals with it.

"It's my fault," she whispers.

"Hey! Don't start thinking like that, kid. You want someone to blame, blame the creep who took you. Blame the corrupt bastards at the PD who turned a blind eye when your mom went asking for you. Blame the scum that did the burning, or the ones who stood by and watched while those folk died. It's their fault because they had a choice. Got that?"

Diana turns to me, her sockets wide. I picture her the way she must have looked before, and my heart breaks a little more. She's just a kid, alone in Hell.

"What do I do now, Nick?"

She lets out a sob that tears through my gut. She's trapped in this place and everyone who knew her, cared about her, has moved on. But that doesn't mean there's no one here for her. I ain't her family, but I'm something. Ruby too.

"Whatever it is, kid, we'll figure it out together. Me and you."

She sniffs, fighting to hold it together. "You mean that?"

I swing my legs off the bed so I'm facing her. I mean what I'm going to say and I want her to know it.

"You say this guy's still out there?"

Diana nods.

"That's good enough for me. We'll find him, we'll make him remember you, then we'll decide what happens to him. The two of us."

"The two of us."

Diana lies back on her bed and rolls on her side to face the wall. Ghosts don't sleep like the living do, but they rest. I guess staring at the cracks in the beige panels is comforting. It's all she knew for sixty years.

I go back to my cell and text Zia again.

Any updates about my office?

I've committed revenge once. My soul's damned. The guy who killed Diana, who got all those folks burned alive, deserves what's coming to him. His hands are bloodier than mine, and that's blood that'll never wash away. Not by all the rain in Hell.

TOMORROW NEVER KNOWS

Morning comes. I think about what Charon said, the way he implied that one day it won't.

Zia hasn't gotten back to me about my office, which means she's working on it. So we wait. It's all me and the kid can do. Truth be told, being stuck in a dingy motel on the city's outskirts ain't all bad. Now I can finally recover from what Michelle Wheeler put me through and digest the new input.

The last few days have proven too interesting, even for me.

It also gives me a little respite from the growing list of folk following me. Butler and Gavin, Marvin Clancy, Charon, the Amarok, whatever the Hell is in that mist, and that other presence I feel wherever I go. The more I think about the latter, the more I'm convinced that lingering sensation of being followed is something new. Something that hasn't revealed itself yet.

The weight I feel when it's close is familiar. I felt it last night at Redwood and Maine. If it meant me or Diana harm, it had its chance to act after Charon disappeared. I can only hope its inaction is a good thing.

The Ferryman and the cops I can deal with. Neither's

gonna act now. Charon just wants to see the Fateless meet his end. Henry and Lori? Well, they've been up my ass like a suppository for years and it don't worry me all that much, now Ruby's cleaned up the Wheeler place. I know her friends will have left the place spotless, so as far as the PD can prove, I'm clean. Nothing to hide.

That leaves Marv and the fog, and whatever's inside of it. If Harry still lived, I'd call him, give him the skinny, and he'd figure this all out while the coffee was brewing. Never met anyone who knew more about Hell than him.

Demons and fallen angels don't count. Not exactly reliable.

Asking him ain't an option anymore. Never will be again. I need to do my own homework from now on, stop muddling through shit, expecting I'll come out on top. That's a dangerous game, and I'm not in any rush to find out what Charon's plan is for the Fateless.

We're still in the motel room. Diana's watching cartoons on the TV. Maybe parenting isn't all that hard after all.

"Kid? I'm just stepping out for a spell. You okay?"

She waves a hand at me, glued to the screen. She's got a lot of catching up to do. I reckon it takes her mind off the revelations of the night before. God knows she needs it. It's all His fault, if you ask me.

The motel's split-level, and I lean on the balcony rail overlooking the forecourt with one, lonely car parked below. I've seen a few places like this in my time. Used to use them a lot in my first life, tailing all sorts of folks, looking for dirt anywhere I could. Any time I followed someone into one of these places, I knew a payday wasn't far behind.

The pine forest outside the city stretches for miles. Sun's rising over the trees, and Hell's looking mighty pretty from where I'm standing. I light a cigarette and enjoy a moment of peace. Almost, but not quite, I can ignore the ghost dangling from the roof, legs swaying all gentle-like.

Wonder if the poor sucker hung himself, or if something more nefarious happened. Chances of either are fair in a joint like this.

Wonder what kind of creature calls that forest home. Demons, I reckon. It's secluded, vast, thick. They'd love it there. A cult, maybe? Seen that before. They love a motel by some trees. Travelling salesmen and sex workers. Perfect sacrifices.

"Harry and Maeve, they'd know." A sigh rips out of me. "They knew everything."

I take a deep drag from my cigarette and wipe away the stray tear that had the guts to leak from my eye. Not that there's anything wrong with crying, but I gotta keep myself strong for the kid.

And I'm gonna keep telling myself that.

In my pocket, the cell vibrates. Fishing it out, I feel my pulse quicken when I see a new text from Zia. About time. Before I can open it, someone calls. My pulse breaks into a sprint.

It's Rosa. Date must've gone swell. I don't want to fuck up the fine work I did just last night, so I answer before checking the message.

"Hey, I know you said you were going to call me, but so soon?"

A pause.

"I am afraid Ms. Riberio is unable to speak just now, Mr. Holleran."

Marvin Clancy. Using Rosa's cell. Without a doubt in my mind, I know I'm gonna kill that bastard.

"You lay one fucking hand—"

"Now, now, Mr. Holleran. Let us be frank with one another. You know very well I had to use force to subdue your woman after she came looking for me. Ms. Riberio followed me home in the taxi you *put her in. Brave, but foolish. I have not harmed her more than I had to."*

I pound my fist against the balcony rail. "She came looking for you?"

"It seems your act of bravado at the restaurant only served to pique her interest. You are lucky. Even knowing the danger she was in, she only warned me to stay away from you. She must care a great deal for you. But make no mistake, it is you *I want. Once I have what I want, once I have Lucifer, she will be immaterial to me. That is why it is in all of our best interests that you do as I say."*

"You want Lucifer, huh?" My words are thick, fast. A snarl. "I can't do it, you crazy bastard. Even if I *wanted* to. Wheeler's ritual had so many moving parts, I wouldn't even know where to start. The only two people who *might* have known are gone."

Another pause and I can hear muffled crying in the background. It makes my vision go black around the edges, makes my body itch to do something. Anything.

"The Devil will come, Mr. Holleran. He does not want harm to befall you."

"You're out of your goddamn mind."

"I believe I will be vindicated. You will receive GPS coordinates on your cell from Rosa's number. Arrive alone, tonight, after dark. No police, no assistance. If I see anyone else, Ms. Riberio dies. And remember, I can see just as well as you can. I will not hurt her if I do not have to, but do you believe I will?"

"Yes." There's no doubt in my mind.

"Very good. I wish we could have conducted business in a more progressive manner. Remember that this is all your fault. Be seeing you. Alone."

The call ends and I squeeze the cell so hard I think it's gonna snap. It vibrates again. The GPS coordinates. Rosa's way out of town, in the countryside surrounding Haven City. Somewhere in that forest. Guess I know what lurks out there now.

I march back to the motel room, jam the cell in my pocket and throw the door open.

"Come on, kid. We're leaving. I messed up, big time. Rosa's in trouble."

...

Another cab ride leaves me cursing that I didn't take my Mustang last night, though with the speed I wanted to travel, I'd have cops on my tail for sure. Last thing I need is a trip to the station, and you can bet your bottom dollar that Butler and Gavin would get involved.

We head for The Styx. I need to speak to Ruby. With no Harry or Maeve, she's my go-to now. Lucky her.

I need to prepare. Can't head to Marv's location with

just my Ruger and a head full of steam. Fortunately, she'll have what I need. Each night since the Wheelers' place and my meeting with Lucifer, that goddamn mist has appeared, hiding something dangerous inside. I'd be a fool if I thought tonight would be different. I'm no use to Rosa if I die before I reach her.

By the time the cab pulls up outside The Styx, it's early afternoon. Diana's patting my hand. Has she been doing that all the way here? Maybe, I just haven't noticed. With all the thoughts running amok in my head, I didn't even consider sending Ruby a message to make sure she's around, though I can count the times I've seen her outside the bar on one hand. If the joint's open, she's there.

It's a hot day, like the sun's trying its damnedest to remind us of summers gone-by, or maybe my boiling blood's keeping me warm. Despite that, there ain't many out on the streets. Haven's usual bustle lulls. Maybe it's the muggy weather, but my gut tells me it's something else. I glance around at the living, passing by on the sidewalk. Most trudge with their heads down, avoiding eye-contact. Pale faces, tight with anger, others blank with inertia.

For a moment, I listen to my city, peer at it with open eyes. Haven—Christ, Hell for all I know—feels sick. Rotten.

"You sense it, too," Diana says, those wide pits staring up at me.

I nod. "Feels like I'm about to walk into a room full of armed gangsters with just a toothpick for protection."

"Something's coming, Nick. It's not just Marvin. It's something else. I don't know how to explain it, but I'm scared."

I hold out my hand and she takes it. "Me too, kid. Me too. But first things first, huh?"

The upstairs of The Styx looks empty as we duck in out of the daylight. Blinking, my sight adjusts, and I see Guz standing behind the bar where he always is, cleaning some already sparkling glasses.

"Ruby here?" I ask, and head towards the stairs leading to the basement without waiting for an answer.

He bobs his head once without so much as looking at me. To be honest, I don't think I've ever heard the dude speak. Shame. I'll bet he has some stories. I take the steps two-at-a-time, so fast I hurtle through the tasteful, shimmering beads that separate the stairwell from the lower Styx, sending them swinging.

"Jesus H Christ," Ruby shouts, as I explode into sight. "Will a day go by where I don't see your sorry ass?"

I glance around. Several ghosts linger near the stage, and by the jukebox, tapping his foot along to the outlaw radio sounds, is Waylon, an old cowboy ripped right from the Wild West. How he ended up in Portland beats me, but I like the guy. To hear him tell it, he must have run across most of the famous faces of the era—Billy the Kid, Doc Holiday. Hell, he says he met his end when Wyatt Earp himself ran him outta Tombstone and his horse took a wrong turn into a canyon. He glances over at me when he hears Ruby's yell and grins, his teeth appearing beneath his thick, grey moustache.

"Hey, bucko. Think you can help me over here?"

He's pointing at the jukebox. *Vamos* by The Pixies. Wish I had the time to appreciate his choice. I slip in a quarter and give him a nod.

"Catch you later, Waylon."

Nice fella.

Diana's headed over to the bar. Ruby smiles down at her. I follow, and that motherly look disappears as soon as she lays eyes on me.

"What am I now, your secretary?" Ruby asks, as I lean against the bar.

I don't take a seat. I ain't staying. I've already wasted more time here than I wanted. Selecting songs for a dead cowboy wasn't what I came here to do.

"That skin-walker, Jim, said you wanted him to leave details of a case you discussed with me, like you don't have your own office. Although, for the record, he seemed pretty shook up. I told you we were getting Wendigo sightings around these parts. Maybe it's time you looked into it."

"When I can. Remember Marvin Clancy?" Something in my voice wipes the scowl from her face. "He's got Rosa."

"Shit." Rubes slaps a hand against the counter. "What the Hell for?"

"He wants me," I reply, pointing at myself with both index fingers, "and shit-for-brains here didn't put an end to his nonsense early enough. He turned up at Tony's last night, in the middle of our date. I played the danger down for Rosa because I didn't want to ruin her evening and she went snooping around after him. Now he's using her to get to me."

"What do you need, Nick?"

I want to reach out and hug the lady, but I'll need to put a pin in it until someone's life isn't in danger.

"I'm pretty low on supplies and I don't know what

Marv's capable of, other than that he can take a toilet to the face pretty damned well. There's something else too. Creatures in the mist that forms out of nowhere, the last two nights. They're stalking me. I need holy water, bullets, a crucifix, Battenspurgers and Expungers. I don't wanna walk in there unprepared."

Ruby bites her lip, stares at the ceiling. I can see her doing an inventory in her mind. She sighs.

Now, in my experience, that's not the best kind of reaction when you're asking for help.

"Shit, I don't have much, but I'll give you what I can. There's holy water, a handful of bullets, and I'll give you my crucifix." She pulls a necklace over her head with a palm-sized iron cruciform dangling from it. "But I only have one Battenspurger, and no Expungers. Sorry, Nick. That's it."

I take the necklace, the metal cool against my palm, as she grabs a clear bottle from under the counter and places it in front of me. Holy water. Rubes always keeps a supply of it. It's an excellent deterrent for rowdy ghosts and demons. I run through my updated inventory. It ain't great. Not a disaster either, mind.

"Thanks, Rubes. I owe you... What, three times now?"

"Nick, at this stage, I think I'm taking it as a given you can't pay me back." She smiles, but I can tell it's forced and it soon slips from her face. "Listen, with no Expunger, you know what that means, right?"

"I better not run into any ghosts that need a severe ass-kicking?"

"Ha-fucking-ha. It means you can't kill Marvin Clancy. Nick, he's a Devil Worshipper, and he understands

Hell. If you kill him, you'll have to deal with his ghost right away, else he'll cause more trouble dead than alive, and you can't stop that without an Expunger. Think before you act. Please?"

Shit. Well, best laid plans and all that. To be honest, 'kill Marvin Clancy' wasn't much of one.

I'm glad Ruby spelled it out for me, because I hadn't considered it. I could've marched in there, like the Wheeler place not two nights ago, and let the bat right out of Hell. I don't have the time to go hunting fae to make an Expunger either. If I did, my luck would bring Queen Lilith down on my ass quicker than you can say Tuatha de Danann.

"Sure thing, boss. Got that Battenspurger?"

Ruby disappears into the back room then returns with a small, metallic egg. She holds it between her index finger and thumb, grabs a handful of napkins, wraps it up and lays it on the counter. She tosses me a magazine for the Ruger, too. Ruby's good people. I pocket the 'egg', tucking it inside my jacket, patting it down, but not too hard.

Gotta be careful with the Battenspurger. See, it may look like metal, but it ain't. Battenspurgers break, and when they do...oh, boy. All I'm saying is, you don't wanna be anywhere close when that thing goes off.

"One more thing," I say, flicking my head at Diana, who's perched herself on a barstool nearby. "Keep an eye on her."

The kid lets out a squawk. "What? No way. I'm coming! I can help."

I meet her hollow sockets. There's no doubt she could help me, but Marvin's instructions were pretty clear. "Diana, he'll know I didn't come alone. He can see you, remember? And you've sensed the things out there. Even if he doesn't have some way to hurt you—and as a Devil Worshipper, it ain't likely—those monsters might. He's already got Rosa. I can't let him harm you too. Being dead doesn't mean you're immortal."

She bows her head. I reach out and give her shoulder a comforting squeeze.

"Will you come back?" she asks.

"Yes," I say. "We've got a job to do, remember?"

They always say 'don't make promises you can't keep', but I'll die trying.

Diana throws herself forward, and wraps those washed-out arms around my neck, rocking me back with the force. The barstools behind me shift backwards, and only Ruby's reflexes stop the bottle of holy water from spinning off the bar. Man, this kid's got so much power I almost reconsider bringing her with me. Almost.

I pry my neck free of her frigid grip.

"See you soon, kid."

Snatching up the holy water, I nod at Ruby and make my way upstairs. It's odd, I ain't been alone in days, and going up those stairs I feel like I'm missing my skin. Guz ignores me as I pass him by and emerge into the sunlight, dazzled by the glare.

As I'm stood in the doorway, I feel it. That unseen weight pressing on me, against my chest, a too-cold breeze on my skin.

"I've had enough of this crap," I mutter, patting my jacket down, thinking fast.

Letting whatever's watching me think I've stepped out for a smoke but forgot my cigarettes, I scowl and head back inside. Throwing a finger up against my lips in Guz's direction—like I need to, dude wouldn't say boo to a...forget about it—I barrel past the chairs and tables towards the stage, and slide under it.

Then, I wait.

It's worth a shot, right?

My hunch pays off. The door of The Styx swings open and in strides the unmistakable form of Suraz. He pauses, glances around, and I feel that pressure again for a moment as I shuffle back into the shadows. The Nephilim nods at Guz, who must have cleaned every glass in this place six times and has moved onto his seventh, then strides downstairs.

Why the fuck is Suraz following me? My guardian angel? Or something else?

Guess I'll find out tonight. He's not let me out of his sight in two days, and I aim to misbehave. Marv said to come alone, but it's not like I can tell a fucking Nephilim to stay away.

All I need is long enough that Marv thinks I'm playing by his rules. Once Suraz figures out he's lost me, he'll track me down again pretty quick. Then he can play his part. My ace in the hole.

I hope.

Climbing out from under the stage, I dust myself down—and ensure the Battenspurger's intact—then make myself scarce. As I jog down the sidewalk, my cell vibrates in my pocket. Another message from Zia. Reading her first escaped my mind.

I flick it open, and read the information, my eyes growing wider with each word. She's got the name of the guy who lived in my office when Diana died. His date of birth, his family details and his occupation. Still running, I dial her number. She answers before the first ring's out.

"Much obliged, Zia. I owe you one. Tell me, this guy still alive?"

She laughs. *"Alive and kicking, unless you thought I omitted his death date for a joke."*

I try to keep my breathing steady. Running and talking's tough, and I ain't as young as I used to be. "I don't always get your sense of humor."

"Can I assume that, if you're asking if he's still alive, you want to speak to him?"

"Oh, I'd *love* to speak to him. Can I get an address? I'll let you know how it goes. Thanks, Zia. Pretty sure there's a story in this."

"Hey, maybe it's one I can actually print this time."

I hang up and pause to catch my breath. As I do, Zia's message arrives and I scan the address she sends. It's the name that keeps drawing my eye.

I know that name. I really don't believe in coincidences.

A DAY IN THE LIFE

The chair crashes to the floor, taking me with it. The landing knocks the wind out of me, but I'm still trapped. My captor turns and, without pause, pulls me upright, chair and all, like I weigh as much as a ragdoll.

The ropes binding my wrists and ankles bite into my flesh. The whimper that escapes my throat is genuine. I'm defenseless, powerless, small. Worse, I'm on the verge of panic. Whatever he's planning for me, for Nick, can only be bad.

Why did I follow this creep? Because I knew Nick had gotten in way over his head? Because I can't ignore a mystery? Because I wanted to pay him back for the time we've wasted?

He made an effort. Some part of me thought I should too.

Dumb, Rosa. Real dumb. Next time, pay him back by getting dinner.

Marvin Clancy leers at me, the ragged cut across his forehead weeping blood down his wide face. Nick's handiwork, I'm pretty sure. He hasn't even bothered to patch it shut. Those black eyes of his bore into mine and I shiver.

"I do hope Mr. Holleran comes through for you, Ms. Riberio. Either way, this will all be over soon enough."

He moves away, back to the book he's reading on the table. His back is to me, for all the good it does when I can't get free. The book's an ancient, leather-bound thing, like nothing I've ever worked with at the library, and he's engrossed in the ritual it details.

Damn it, Nick. Why didn't you tell me he was a Devil Worshipper? *Always keeping secrets. When I get my hands on you...*

No, that's not fair. I wanted him to let me in, tell me about his case. The old Nick would have lied at the restaurant, slunk off to the restroom without telling me about his trouble, then let me go home none the wiser. He'd have already been pulling away and I'd have lost him again without even realizing.

Instead, I'm trapped in a cabin in the woods with a lunatic who can lift me without even trying. But the strength isn't what terrifies me most. It's those eyes. Cold and black.

Until he talks about Nick. Then they change. One second, anger; the next, a feverish passion burns in them. I don't want to rile him up. He hasn't hurt me, and I hope to keep it that way.

I've dealt with men like him before and they prefer women scared, but not hysterical. They desire control. Power. I screamed so much when he caught me at his place that he gagged me, and only untied me once the tears stopped and I promised I wouldn't yell, his meaty fists bunched up, knuckles white. Then he brought me here.

Wherever here is.

"Don't know why you think Nick will come," I gasp, voice shrill and wavering in my ears.

I've seen crazy people snap before, and I'm alone here. If he does...

No, I can't think about that. Not now.

"We hadn't spoken in years. Whatever we might have had, it's not there anymore. I'm not the leverage you want."

"Do not underestimate yourself. I'm sure seeing you again has rekindled the old flame. He *will* come."

He puts the book down, leaving it open on the table. It's written in symbols I don't recognize and there's a silver eye on the cover that freaks me out when I glance at it, like it's staring back at me, through my eyes and into my soul.

"He sounded concerned for your well-being when we spoke. Perhaps you are underestimating his affection for you? I have watched Mr. Holleran for some time. I know his character. When he arrives, which he will, and does what I need him to do, you may leave. I will have no further use for you."

"I *may* leave? Like there's a better option on the table?"

Marvin turns those cold eyes on me. He's huge, so big his head brushes the rafters of the tiny log cabin. I'm thankful he lit a fire, though it wasn't for my benefit. He's preparing a ritual, he says. Chalk pentagrams and etchings cover the floor and walls and a part of me regrets ever meeting Nick Holleran.

Except that he'd have died if we'd never met, and no matter what he says, there's something sacred in life. I believe that all the more when Marvin looms over me. This man would kill in the blink of an eye. He has. I recognize a predator.

"If you remain here, you will bear witness to the Father. You will bask in his presence. Even one as sightless as you could not miss him."

"I don't see why meeting your father would make me wanna stay."

The words escape my lips before I can pull them back. A nervous quip, the panic filling up my chest and flooding my brain, slipping off my tongue. One of the things I missed about Nick since the last time we were together. He never seemed to be without a line, and he appreciated one in return.

I can usually swallow them at the wrong moments, unlike him, but right now my thoughts, and mouth, are all over the place.

If I'd been thinking straight, I'd never have been stupid enough to get myself into this mess. Nick and me, we're both in danger, and it's all my fault.

I wince as Marvin takes a step closer, but he drops to his haunches, a wide smile on his face that doesn't reach his soulless eyes.

"Not *my* father, Ms. Riberio. He is nothing but a disappointment. To me, to you, even to the merciful God he was so pathetically enamored with. He spent most of his meaningless life in service to the deity who put us all in Hell to begin with. Fitting for such a meek, unremarkable man. I am speaking about Lucifer. When Mr. Holleran arrives and provides his assistance, we will meet Lucifer. The true Father. We exist in his realm and long have I desired to pledge myself to his service. I have accomplished much through my studies, devoted myself to him from the moment my first death opened my eyes. When I meet the Father, my life's work can finally, truly begin."

I knew Marvin's elevator didn't go up to the penthouse, but staring into the man's face, I realize he's unhinged. Nick told me about Hell—an obsession with him, and me acting as his therapist often drove a wedge between us—but the intensity with how Marvin talks about it is something else. Does Nick deal with people like him all the time?

His world is something I'm not sure I can handle and I tried to throw myself into it headfirst. I thought I was ready.

Nick always kept me at arm's length when it came to his cases, but he doesn't always see the full picture. He told me he'd warned Marvin off last night, but as my taxi passed him, I saw the look on his face. I knew he'd come for Nick, and I wanted to stop him. Find out where he lived and call the police, tell them about the stalking, warn him off myself if I had to.

God, I want to scream, cry, beg. But I know it won't help. I'm here until he has Nick.

I lower my eyes and shrink backwards, the only protection I can give myself if Marvin flips.

Keep him talking. He's a narcissist. A man with a plan. He wants *everyone to see how special he is.*

"What does Nick have to do with Lucifer?"

I'd have thought the Devil was a little above Nick's pay grade. What would the ultimate evil want with a Haven P.I.?

Marvin leans forward, forcing a flinch out of me. He smells...too clean. Like a crime scene after it's been bleached. Sweat pours from his face, mixing with the blood oozing from his wound. A watery-red bead drops from the tip of his nose and lands on my lap. He's so close. It's like he's backing me up without moving me, and I hate getting pushed into a corner.

"Because he won't have a choice. I believe Lucifer, for reasons known only to him, is protecting Mr. Holleran. Since his rebirth, he has been so unremarkable, stumbling through Hell with his eyes half-closed. Then, two days ago, the Father visited him. Now, his Nephilim follow him. There are ways to summon Lucifer, but I have no wish to put him in my thrall. I am not worthy of that. Instead, I wish to serve and take my place at his feet. But the Father's interest in the detective presents me with an opportunity. My friends will put Mr. Holleran's life in danger. If that does not work, it will force me to harm you until he relents and summons the Father himself. He says he cannot, but I do not believe him. If he refuses, I will kill him; a long, slow death. If nothing else, that will catch Lucifer's attention."

I snarl, throwing my head forward with as much force as I can muster. My forehead crunches into his nose. I feel bone and cartilage flatten. Marvin staggers backward and the momentum carries me with him. I crash to the floor again, face-first this time. I can only twist my head so my cheek bears the brunt. Pain explodes in my jaw, but the ragged gasps I hear from Marvin make it all worth it.

I tense, expecting a kick or punch as he climbs to his feet. Instead, the room lurches as Marvin picks up the chair and sets me straight for the second time. I cringe, shrink back and screw my eyes shut, expecting a beating.

Maybe I shouldn't have done anything, but I need to get out of this chair and away from him. He says he won't harm me, but after he's killed Nick, why *wouldn't* he kill me too? I'm a loose end.

And he'll need someone to take his anger out on when Lucifer doesn't appear.

The seconds stretch, but all I hear is the wet, ragged breaths of my captor.

I crack an eye open. Marvin's standing at the table again, book in hand. Purple blotches swell below his eyes and dark crimson streams from his ruined nose, but if he's in pain, his eyes don't show it. They don't show any emotion, for that matter.

Blood pours onto his white shirt now, cascading from his beaten face. Without even trying to staunch the flow, he sets the book down and unbuttons his sodden shirt. He throws it aside but my gaze is stolen by the sight of his bare torso.

Marvin's heavyset, but a thick layer of muscle sits below the flab, giving his torso and arms a thick, sturdy look. But that's not what's making panic begin to bubble up inside me, set the tears streaming down my face. His skin's covered with tattoos—copies of the pentagrams and etchings from around the cabin in a multitude of colors—and they're writhing across his skin like a horrific, living piece of art.

Above his heart are angry tally marks, like he cut himself with a knife. So many of them.

"What are they?" I ask, unable to help myself. "Those marks?"

Marvin glances down at them, face impassive. "A reminder of the souls I have taken to further my studies." He lays a thick finger beside the first one. "This is my mother, I took her first, the day I was reborn. I was ten."

"You k-killed her?" I stammer, the taste of salt thick on my lips as the tears stream down my face. "You killed *all* of them? You're a *monster!*"

"It is almost time," he says, turning away from me and approaching the door. "My friends are hungry."

Through the cabin's windows, I see darkness falling. Martin stands in the doorway, mumbling to himself, arms stretched wide. The muscles in his back tremble under the fat.

"What are you doing?" I cry, straining against my restraints.

I have to get out of here, warn Nick somehow. This evil... I can taste it on my tongue, smell it in the air, like the cabin's steeped in it. The words spilling out of Marvin's mouth are the source of it all. It's all coming from him.

He pauses and turns. The grin that splits his face is almost as horrifying as the red glow in his eyes.

"I'm calling my friends, Ms. Riberio, and the mist that carries them. I learned this trick a long time ago. You see, I may not be worthy to control the Father, but the lesser denizens of Hell are mine to dominate."

He peers out into the fog and I can still hear the smile in his voice.

"We are going to welcome Mr. Holleran to his destiny, you and I."

DON'T LET ME DOWN

The GPS location Marv supplied leads me to a place in the middle of nowhere. I follow the route as far as I can in the Mustang until the road turns impassable. Then I sit behind the wheel for five minutes, trying to muster the courage to make the rest of the trip on foot. GPS says I've still got a mile to go, through dense forest with no trail. And the mist is back. Imagine my enthusiasm.

My gut tells me this mist is somehow Marvin Clancy's doing. The silent drive gave me the chance to turn a few things over in the old skull and I realized, each time the mist appeared, I've run into Marv. At first, I couldn't see that. Charon, the Amarok and that watching presence confused the matter. But I've run into the Ferryman without the mist, and now I know Suraz's the one keeping an eye on me, only Lucifer knows why.

So that leaves Marv. He must have been in Meadow Park that first night, before rocking up at the Styx. He tailed me at Tony's, and now, with the fog thick at the location he gave me, it can only mean one thing—he's controlling it. The creatures inside it too, logic says. Coincidence can kiss my skinny ass.

If I didn't already know it, I'd say Marvin Clancy is one dangerous sonofabitch.

I carry out one last check. My Ruger's loaded and I've doused the bullets with holy water. The spare magazine's in my waistband, the Battenspurger's intact and I've got Ruby's crucifix in my pocket.

"Only one thing for it, Nick," I say to myself, staring into the rearview. Frightened eyes look back. Can't blame myself, really. I screw the top off the bottle of holy water and pour the remaining liquid over myself. I'll take any extra edge I can. "You ready? You better be."

The Mustang's door cuts through the mist as I open it, the thick fog oozing back into place as I swing it shut. I've left the engine running in case I come through this and need a quick getaway. The headlamps seem dull in the gloom. Grey surrounds me; can't even see the night sky. Pulling out the Ruger, I hold my cell in front of me like a compass and follow the route to its end. My boots squelch in the sodden earth.

Ahead of me, a black spot forms. A shadow looms out of the fog; a deep darkness that the mist won't touch. I ain't surprised.

"Death lays at the end of your path, Fateless," Charon says, his voice like two tombstones rubbing against each other.

"Thought you couldn't see my end, Ferryman," I hiss, stooping with the Ruger held out in front of me. Did I just hear snuffling?

"True, and I hope my business here includes you, but another's end calls me here this night."

"Well, shit."

As far as I know, there's only two other people in this part of the forest—Rosa and Marv. Can't kill the latter, since I've got no way to deal with his spirit. Battenspurger might buy me time, but I'd need to get Rosa out first. If either of us get caught in the blast radius, we'd get blown to pieces.

If it comes to it, I'll kill Marv to save Rosa, and deal with the consequences later. I guess you can call that my M.O.

A scream pierces the night, filled with rage, pain and unspeakable loss. It makes my bones shake, and when another howls in reply, I almost turn on my heel and flee. The mist distorts distance, but in front of me, red lights pierce through the fog, edges bleeding into the vapor.

Flesh... Fresh blood... Sweet, sweet meat... It calls to us... So hungry... It gnaws... Stop the pain... Feed us... Free us... Your body, so strong, so whole... Give it to us...

The mist billows out like a curtain in front of me as the horror emerges. It looks like a yak, hideous and twisted. Red eyes glow. Saliva drips from its maw and sizzles on the unseen ground beneath its hooves. Its fur's matted, bare in places, and bone juts out through skin. And its face... Surrounding those crimson eyes is a skull with slithers of flesh and shavings of fur stuck to it.

It howls at me. My ears ring and I fight against covering them, keeping my Ruger trained on it.

Another creature appears behind it. A bear, I reckon. Or it used to be.

"Fateless, have you ever faced Wendigo? Dangerous foes. I believe I will witness your end tonight after all."

Well, Jim, mystery fucking solved. If I make it through this, I'm collecting a fee from the skin-walker and his goddamned clan. Reckon I'll deserve it.

"Fuck you, Charon," I mutter, as the second Wendigo draws up beside the first. "You knew from the first night? A little heads up wouldn't have killed you."

I glance at the Ferryman and he grins, features fading into the darkness until the mist curls around him like a cloak. Gone.

My hair, already wet from the holy water, drips liquid down my forehead. My clothes stick to me from the moisture in the air. The mist seems alive, swirling and gathering thicker around me. Gentle as I can, I reach into my jacket and pull out the Battenspurger, shedding napkins into the wet leaves.

The yak Wendigo cocks its head.

"We smell your fear, human... Give in..."

The way its jaws move when that piercing, high-pitched voice comes out will give me nightmares for years. Assuming I have years.

I squeeze the trigger. A bullet punches into the yak's forehead. Steam sizzles from the entry wound and a squeal bursts from its mouth. I fire again, this time at the bear, two quick shots that thud into the ruin of its body. Their screams are too human for comfort—tortured, filled with a bone-deep fear, a desperate need for release. The spirits possessing these animals were people a long time ago, but now they're puppets too. Another crime Marv's gonna pay for.

I still need to put them down. Rabid animals with rabid minds.

The bullets only bought me time; they won't put down something as wicked as a Wendigo. To be honest, I'm not sure what will, but God loves a lost cause, right? I throw the Battenspurger overarm. Before it impacts, I turn, determined to put some space between me and the detonation.

I slip in the mud.

Crashing to the ground, I spin as the Battenspurger explodes. The light sears my vision. I make myself small, curling into a ball as the Wendigo howl in frustration and pain. The grenade obliterates ghosts, even if they form again later. Their bodies straight-up burst all over the forest. Chunks of flesh pelt me, the stench of rotted yak and bear fur thick in my nose, the splatter of their ichor on my skin. The night falls silent. Pushing onto my elbow, I glance around.

The mist's still thick, but no Wendigo. Lights dance in my vision, though blinking doesn't force them away. In fact, the colors are shimmering, moving together and swirling when I look at them. It's then I realize my mistake.

Battenspurgers destroy matter, force ghosts apart, but don't kill them.

Wendigo aren't the creatures; they're the malevolent spirits inside, and I just ripped them from their bodies. One rushes at me, and all I can do is lay there in the mud.

"Well, fuck me."

The Wendigo rushes into me, and my body turns hot, and I mean fucking hot. It's like I've burst into flame, sizzling like pork rind. Then the specter attempting to possess me howls in pain and scatters away. Another hurtles at me and I feel a slight chill before the fire returns. A moment later that Wendigo retreats too.

I pat myself down, trying to figure it out, and then realize I'm soaked, but not with sweat.

"The holy water," I mutter. "Guess it was a good idea to go for the full baptismal after all."

The Wendigo spirits flee into the mist. I scramble to my feet, trying to brush the mud from my clothes, but all I do is move it around a little. Before I can congratulate myself on surviving a battle with Wendigo, I hear more screams, snuffling, baying. Red lights appear in the mist.

Those first two were just the vanguard, and all I have left is bullets. The holy water might prevent them from possessing my body until it dries, but nothing will stop them tearing me limb from limb.

Should have waited to use the shittin' Battenspurger.

The amount of eyes glaring at me, swimming and swirling, blazing crimson, refusing to stick to one position, disorient me. I swing my gun arm around, looking for something—anything—to unload my clip at. Then something collides with me from behind and I fire, reflex. Claws pierce my skin and teeth bite at my hamstrings. I fall forwards, twisting as I do, and fire a couple of rounds into the snarling, fever-ridden terrier trying to feast on my thigh.

A missing dog.

The bullets slam it off its feet with a snarl. It rolls and gathers itself to leap at my face. It's so close I can see the collar around its neck and the name etched into the metal tag. Rufus. Never thought a Rufus would tear my throat out.

I fire again, and the Ruger clicks. Out of bullets. Of all the things in Hell, a possessed ankle-biter of a dog's gonna kill me.

I wonder how long it'll take me to spring Awareness and Strengthen when my heart stops pumping blood and my brain flickers out. Even dead, I'm never gonna stop coming for Marvin fucking Clancy.

A golden blade cuts through the mist, straight through the canine's neck. Its body thrashes around, the Wendigo spirit caught inside it. I follow the sword upwards and thank Lucifer that his Nephilim followed me here. I hoped he would and my guardian angel, my ace in the hole, didn't let me down.

Even if he left it late. Nearly too late.

"Run, Nick Holleran," Suraz says, that familiar weight settling on me as he meets my eyes. Right now, it's a comfort. "I will hold them at bay."

A memory flashes in my mind. Suraz at the Styx after he hauled my ass in there; his face, armor and sword covered in gore. *He* fought the Wendigo and the Amarok in Meadow Park.

He really does care!

"Can't." Pain lances through my back and shredded hamstring as I struggle to my feet. The blood trickling down my skin feels hot in the icy fog. "Gotta save Rosa from that sonofabitch Devil Worshipper. Long story, but all this is coming from him."

Suraz snarls. Another Wendigo hurtles through the mist and the Nephilim moves faster than my eyes can comprehend, spinning and twisting his golden sword in an arc. Another carcass drops to the ground, legs beating and thrashing beside the dog. The Wendigo spirit pushes its way through the canine carcass and Suraz slams his foot down on it. The spirit howls, more rage than anything.

"You were wise to trust in the Almighty's blessing, Nick Holleran. The holy water has kept you safe for now, but enough spirits will overwhelm us both. Go then. I will follow, if I am able. One of us must stop him. If the Devil Worshipper is the source, I fear the Wendigo's attack shan't end until we do."

Poetic, even in the face of peril. That's a Nephilim for ya. I nod and fumble for my cell. The GPS route guiding me.

"Five hundred yards until your destination," the pleasant, computerized voice intones. If only she fucking knew what in holy Hell I'm dealing with.

I stumble forward as I hear screams behind me. Suraz shouts, beating his sword against his armor to draw the Wendigo to him. He gets his wish, because they start to circle with him at the center, and I realize why it's so cold all of a sudden. Our old friend, the Amarok, is there, leader of the pack, only its fur is patchy and its flesh is rotten and its ice crystals are grey and half-melted. Even so, it stands head and shoulders above the other possessed creatures and its eyes blaze with insane hunger.

If the animals are vehicles, that Wendigo is driving a tank.

It roars as it powers into Suraz and all Hell breaks loose behind me. I break into a sprint as best as my battered body can manage.

"Two hundred yards until your destination."

Almost there. I holster the Ruger to keep one hand free as I slip and slide in the mud, thumping into trees and roots as I do. Then, without warning, a cabin looms.

"You have reached your destination."

It looks to be in decent shape. Marv must stay here often. Smoke emits from the chimney, and wooden steps lead to the porch and front door. I press on, ignoring the carnage behind me. If Suraz can hold them off long enough for me to deal with Marv, I can end this. The stairs creak under my feet as I inch towards the door. I draw the Ruger and stow the cell, holding the gun to my chest as I nudge the entrance open.

The door smashes back in my face.

"Ugh!"

It's the only word I can manage as I stagger backwards and sprawl across the porch. The Ruger spins away out of sight.

Marv looms above, his tattooed torso stripped naked. He's covered in dark shapes, and they move. Maybe it's the blood loss or maybe it's my newfound concussion.

"Welcome, Mr. Holleran," Marv says, standing over me. "I see that the Father did not come to save you from the Wendigo. Perhaps he does not feel they are enough of a danger to you. No matter. I am sure we can find something that will get his attention."

He lifts his boot and stamps on my face, kicking me into darkness.

COME TOGETHER

I dream of Scottish terriers chasing me around a forest, yipping and yapping, while Clint Eastwood drinks Budweiser straight from a keg, laughing at my expense while a man I identify as God wrestles Lucifer in the mud.

I've had weirder dreams, but not many.

Then Marvin goddamn Clancy clubs me across the face with the back of his thick hand and I wake up, whiplash in my neck and a gong reverberating in my skull. My face throbs, then my back and leg join in with their own complaints. They're all dying to remind me of the trouble I've caused them tonight. Everyone's a critic.

"Rise and shine, Mr. Holleran."

Those predator's eyes glint with malice. Sweat and blood covers Marv's pale, cratered face. His nose is mangled, and it's fresh. Rosa's doing, I guess. He should have known better. The mist that's dogged my every move these past few days emits from his pores. It's thinner here, but glancing behind him, I can see it trail off under the cabin's closed door.

My heart fills my mouth when I see Rosa tied to a chair behind him. Her eyes are red, skin paler than normal, but she nods to show me she's hanging in there. I test my arms and discover I'm tied down too. A quick glance around tells me I'm in the cabin. Fire's blazing, and there's chalk drawings of dark iconography all over the place.

"Nice place you got here. Marv. Might want to get a real road carved out though. Had to walk the last leg. Give animal control a call too. You taking breakfast orders? Eggs over easy and a side of toast. Don't skimp on the butter."

Just can't help myself sometimes. The quip ain't just the smart ass in me rearing its head; I'm playing for time, holding out for my brain to kick into gear and figure a way to stop Marv, or for Suraz to join us. Only the forest outside is silent and I don't think he's close. A possessed Amarok alone means he's got his hands full, and there were a *lot* of missing posters up at the Styx. Can't bet on the Nephilim to save the day. Even Suraz didn't sound too confident.

Quick as a viper, Marv's arm snaps out, fingers squeezing the air from my throat. I struggle, but what can I do? His grip's like iron.

"I tire of your inanity, Mr. Holleran." He pulls me closer, and the chair rocks onto its front two legs. I gasp for air as our noses almost touch. "Summon Lucifer. Now."

He releases me just as my vision goes black around the edges. The burning in my face subsides as my blood starts to flow again. Anyone ever throttle you? Your first instinct is to check your windpipe's still in one piece. With my hands tied, all I can do is gulp for sweet air.

"You just wanna meet him, Marv? That it? Nah, ain't buying it." Damn, my voice sounds pathetic in my ears. Weak and stretched. I snatch another lungful of oxygen. "What's your angle?"

The tattoos covering Marv's body twist and writhe. Recognize some. Runes for protection, others for domination of spirits, a couple represent Dagon of all things. Guy's into—pardon my French— the occult. Deep into it.

"All I wish is to meet the Father," he says, fever burning behind his hard eyes. "To bask in his presence. To swear myself to him forevermore."

The Father? Gotcha.

"Which one of those tats is Enochian for 'daddy issues'? Must be tough, being named after a father you don't respect. Believe me, I get that. So, should I call you Marvin Clancy...Junior? Because you left that part out when you introduced yourself."

The muscles in his face go slack. See, some folk react that way when they're surprised. Poker face, some call it, but when you know the tell it's just another expression that announces I've rattled the bastard. Sometimes, nothing is just as suspicious as something.

In the corner of my eye, I see Rosa glancing around. While Marv's focused on me, she's looking for anything we can use to escape. Just hope she finds something soon.

"Do not presume to foist your own weakness on me, Mr. Holleran."

Right now, if I had my hands free, I'd reach for a cigarette. Take my sweet time in lighting it too. I'd take in a long fucking drag and blow the smoke into Marv's face. But I don't got `em free, so I grin instead. That lop-sided, charming smile. Behind Marv, Rosa shakes her head, eyes wide.

"Look, I get it, big guy," I begin, raising one eyebrow for good measure as I tell him a half-lie. I didn't mean to dig dirt up on the Devil Worshipper; it just worked out that way. "You're surprised I looked into you? I'm a P.I., Marv. What'd you exp—"

Bang. His first punch knocks the air right outta me and I only just got my breath back. The second snaps my head aside, knocks a tooth loose, fills my mouth with the taste of hot metal as blood oozes from my split gums. He grips my throat again and squeezes. He bares his teeth, a rictus grin, as he chokes the life outta me with both hands, wringing my neck. The edges of my vision turn black again. My face heats up and a rushing sound fills my ears, like being underwater, though I hear Rosa screaming behind it all. And, somehow, the observational part of my brain, the one I reserve for stakeouts and card games, sees the cabin door open just a slither, then close again. Rosa's yelling drowns out any sound.

It doesn't matter. Marv's killing me. My arms and legs respond, fighting against their restraints, ropes eating into my flesh, but my limbs grow weak.

"Stop!" Rosa screams.

No use. Reckon Marv don't hear a thing. His mind's lost to thoughts of his old man. Yeah, I heard about him. A priest and, as it turns out, a sinner. A piece of shit up to his elbows in blood, who turned to the cloth to hide, like so many of those sonsofbitches do.

Hoped to pay him a visit when this situation resolved itself. Chances are looking slim.

My thoughts drift to my parents. I see them, standing over that makeshift grave in the backyard, all those years ago. I remember their faces when they saw me, just a teenager, arriving when I shouldn't, and what I saw in that pit behind them. The rage in my mother's face. The blankness in my father's eyes. Ancient history.

Funny it's my last thought, but a thing like that sticks with you forever. Even if it's something you'd do anything to forget.

It takes me a hot minute to realize Marv's let go. I still feel the force of his fingers on my throat, but I'm gasping for air, guzzling it into my lungs without thinking. Now he grabs my head, and for a moment I reckon he's gonna pop it like a grape.

"I could do it, you know? Kill you right now with my bare hands," he says, soulless eyes boring into mine. I almost pass out. My head lolls to the side when he releases it, the absence of crushing pressure making it spin. And then I see her.

Diana?

I've no idea how the fuck she got to the cabin, but right now, I don't give a single, stinking shit. She's the one that opened the door, Strengthening more and more all the time. She can get Rosa outta here. The kid creeps up behind her as I try not to give the game away, and Rosa gives a start as the ropes that bind her shift and loosen. She won't see who's helping her—God knows what she makes of all this—but I can see her face flood with relief.

I just gotta keep Marv's attention on me.

"Choking's a bully's way to murder, Marv," I croak, my throat burning. "What, you get your kicks throttling folk while they're tied down? Big guy like you shouldn't need ropes to get the job done. How about you let me up and we can go at it, toe-to-toe?"

It's an idle goad, and I'm hoping he'll think I'm desperate. If I tried to take Marv in a fistfight, he'd crush me. But he pulls back a little, runs his thick fingers over the row of tally marks cut into his chest.

Fuck me, Marv's more of a freak than I ever imagined.

"I killed Mother first. I strangled her, but I didn't tie her down. I had to wear long shirts for weeks, the cuts she left. My fingers cramped from squeezing so hard. It pained me to pry them from her pale throat, I held on so long. My father knew, of course. He prayed for my soul, said his sins reflected on me, that God took his retribution that way. But I knew. God did not gaze on me from above. No, not he. Lucifer called me, welcomed me to his embrace if I could only *earn* it. And if you are not willing to help me meet my true Father, I will *force* your compliance. Or did you think Ms. Riberio was only here as bait, Mr. Holleran."

My eyes flick to her. Diana's frozen in place behind her. She knows Marv'll see her as well as I do.

"Wait!" I yell. He pauses, mid-turn. Don't think I've ever been so relieved. "Wait. Okay, yeah. I'll help. You got it. Me and Lucifer, we got an understanding."

Marv grips my chair, the muscles beneath the layer of fat pushing their way through, the tendons in his thick neck popping.

"An understanding? You have an *understanding* with the Father."

He leers at me, thick lips curving into a smirk. Gut instinct, double down, build a story, a narrative, make him believe. But then he starts laughing.

It reveals his true madness. A high-pitched, cackling

giggle, with tears leaking out of those shark-like eyes, his grip so tight on my chair that the wood splits with a crack. For once, I keep my big fucking mouth shut. The laughter stops, like he's flicked a switch.

"Why you?" he snarls, the muscles in his cheeks, eyes, and jaw all twitching.

I've known Marv's crazy since the Styx, but the depth of his madness blows me away. His mind broke when he died, whenever that happened. Bastard never recovered and I feel sick when a pang of sympathy prods at me.

"You're an unremarkable man. A fool muddling his way through Hell, reckless and ignorant, still desperately seeking the approval of the Almighty that forsook us all. I've seen you, counseling the victims, advocating for the weak. Why? Because you think Heaven will still take you?" He slaps his chest, sweat and blood flying off it. "That is not the way, Mr. Holleran. Our Father descended from Heaven to walk amongst us. *He* will bring us salvation. I have sacrificed so many in his honor. I turned my body into a canvas for him, yet you claim he favors you? If the woman means so much to you, I will make you watch as I strip her soul from her mutilated body and bind it to me. Then I will take pleasure in torturing you, and if the Father arrives, I will show my worthiness through the ruination of your fucking corpse."

Marv's bellowing into my face, clutching my biceps so tight they bruise, spitting all over me as he crushes me. I understand how sardines feel getting shoved into those little, old tins. He doesn't even see me anymore as he screams his fury at me.

Just like that, it's happened, like people always warned

me. My mouth's pushed someone over the edge.

A chair explodes over Marv's head. Splinters fly. Free of her restraints, Rosa comes through. Marv can take a hit, but he still goes down with a yelp of pain. Blood pours from his head and down the artwork on his back. Diana flows behind me, starts working at the ropes on my leg.

"Don't wanna sound ungrateful," I shout to her over my shoulder, eyeing Marv on the floor. "But could you go any faster?"

Rosa whacks him again with the shattered chair, but he's getting up quick. And he's pissed.

"You're lucky I'm here at all," Diana bites out.

One hand pops free. On instinct, I reach for my Ruger, but it ain't there. Course it isn't.

"About that..."

"I was with you the whole time. After you tried to ditch me at the Styx, I followed you back home and got in the trunk."

"Remind me to tell you off later."

Marv sweeps Rosa's legs out and she rolls, slapping out on the cabin floor. Before she can get her feet, he grabs her around the neck and tosses her into the wall. Another of my hands pops free and I throw myself forwards, dragging the chair behind me. I grab Marv around his bull neck and hammer on the wound in his skull with my fist. I kick his knees out, slam elbows into his ribs, hit every weak spot I can think of. I try to choke him—a little revenge would be nice—but his tendons jut and it's like trying to strangle a streetlamp. I reckon it's hurting me more than him.

He throws me off with a shrug of his shoulders and I

topple backwards, flattening the chair under my ass.

"Enough!" Marv roars.

He seems torn between the three of us—we've all defied him—then he glares at Diana and lunges.

The kid screams.

The noise is worse than the sound of the Wendigo. It's anger, yes. Fear. Pain. Her voice splits the night, and I'm fortunate I've got my hands free so I can cover my ears.

But Marv? The cry hits him full-blast. He cannons into the wall and the building shakes as Diana's emotional tornado pins the sorry bastard there. Her screams fade, and as she walks past me the restraints on my ankles unravel. I scramble to my feet, running to Rosa, who's nursing a head wound of her own from her collision with the wall.

Diana, hands outstretched, pushes Marv harder against the wall. He grunts in pain, snarls, strains. The force is invisible, but I can *feel* it. This is beyond Strengthened. This is beyond poltergeist. She isn't just throwing open doors or moving TV remotes anymore. Marv's tendons pop all over his torso, but it's no good. Fucker's pinned. This skinny, teenage ghost has got this beast of a man wedged against a wall through nothing more than her will, and dear Lord is that will ferocious. I grab Rosa, and she holds me tight.

"You good?" I ask.

"Think so," she replies, checking her head and pulling away from me. She gawps at Marv, snarling and straining as Diana lifts him off his feet. "What's doing that to him?"

"Friend of mine."

"Right," Rosa says, eyes flicking to the fireplace. Beside

it is a table with my Ruger on it, spare magazine and all. "This wasn't the second date I'd envisioned, but at least it's memorable."

Before I can laugh, Diana screams. Not like before. This time, it's filled with surprise and confusion and anguish. She staggers as Marv drops to the ground. He pulls himself forward, fingernails digging into the floorboards, and Diana backs off. His tattoos are alive, rippling across his bare skin.

I move, throwing myself to the table, my leg, back, stomach, face and neck all protesting, and grab the Ruger. I pop the empty clip and slam the fresh magazine in place. I spin, aiming the gun at Marv.

"Hold it, big guy. It's over. Reckon a bullet to the head would drop you like it would anyone else."

Diana runs over to us. Marv's focus is once again on me. He climbs to his feet, does it slow, his massive size making the cabin appear tiny. Can't get over how big the guy is. Even with the beating he's taken—Rosa's chair shots, the pummeling I gave him, Diana's psychokinetic assault, the blood pumping from his head, washing over his tattooed torso—he still looks primed for action.

"You will not kill me," he snarls, taking a step forward, and he's right. I don't want to.

I've no way to deal with his ghost. My hope rests on Suraz, but it's silent outside. If he dealt with the Wendigo, he'd have come by now. But, if he leaves me no choice, I'll put two hot pieces of lead in his chest and one between his eyes.

I move backward, toward the door, signaling for Rosa and Diana to move with me.

"Killed before," I grunt, taking another step. "Just a couple of nights ago. It's how I met your buddy Lucifer."

I hear faint cries from outside and I pray to God it's the death throes of a Wendigo, but I'm sure they're cries of pain. Goddamn it.

Marv rushes forward a step. I snap my arm down, and put a bullet through his thigh. I expect him to collapse as the blood starts pumping. Instead, his eyes narrow to slits.

"The Father made a mistake," he snarls, uncaring of the smoke curling from the bullet wound in his meaty thigh. "Unlike God, he never claimed to be infallible. But I see now that he does not care for you, and you have wasted my time. I will carve your souls into my chest and enslave your dead friend."

I shift a foot backwards, and I feel something dig into my thigh through my pocket. The crucifix! I glance at the Satanic tattoos on Marv's body, recall the Wendigo spirit's pain when it tried to pass through the holy water into my body, and decide it's worth a short.

As a scream erupts from outside, I lower my voice and talk fast.

"When I say the word, get outside. Got me? Run, don't stop, outta the mist."

I don't wait for an answer. Thrusting my hand into my pocket, I grab Ruby's necklace and charge at Marv.

"Now!" I scream, and leap at him.

We collide and tumble to the floor. As we fall, I jam the crucifix against his forehead. It sizzles, burning his flesh. He shrieks, eyes rolling, veins bulging. Unlike the bullet wound, this is more than physical pain, He's painted evil on his skin and let it into his soul, and the holiness wants to purge it all.

I press my palm against it—the metal white-hot— holding the iron cruciform in place. My screams rise with his as the flesh under my hand blisters and cracks. Maybe my brush with Lucifer means the cross ain't too keen on me either. Marv's fist slams into my ribs, but I hold on. I swallow the agony as he sinks another punch into my torso. A third.

"Won't you fucking give up?" I snarl, and go to slam the Ruger on his head.

A mistake.

My balance shifts, and Marv unleashes a flurry of hammer blows, forcing me off and sending my gun spinning across the floor. I roll as he kicks me away. With a cry of fury, he rips the crucifix from his head, and throws it into the fireplace. The flames surge and roar when it tumbles through them. He climbs to his feet and I sag against the floorboards, closing my eyes so I don't see Charon grinning at me.

I know it's my end. I only hope Rosa and the kid took my advice.

"Does he come?" Marv asks, his voice child-like and small. Almost a whisper, swallowed by the roaring flames. "You are his messenger, are you not?"

I open my eyes. His ruined, half-melted face is filled with wonder as he stares beyond me. I roll on one side with a groan so I can see what's got Marv so enraptured.

"Took your fucking time," I grumble, sinking back to the ground.

The Nephilim cometh to save the day.

Suraz stands in the doorway, caked in ichor, black

wings of shadow open wide, armor broken and hanging loose in places. He staggers, leaning on his golden sword, obsidian skin and bright eyes standing out against the mist. Even wounded, his presence is undeniable, a weight forcing us all to notice. Rosa and Diana are still inside the cabin—of course they didn't listen—and they both stare at Suraz, mouth agape.

Even an Unawakened can see a Nephilim in battle-mode.

"You meddle with things beyond your comprehension, Devil Worshipper," Suraz hisses, hefting his mighty blade. "One such as you is but an insect beneath Lucifer's boot."

The Nephilim surges at Marv, and then, through the door, I see it. Disaster approaches. The warning dies in my throat; it doesn't even have time to reach my lips.

Charging, committed to the attack, Suraz spins and throws out a wing, sheltering Rosa and Diana. The Wendigo Amarok—hacked all to Hell, missing half its snout and a huge chunk of flank, but still kicking—charges up the porch stairs, roaring a fury, and demolishes the cabin's front as it crashes through the doorway. It mauls Suraz, jaws clamping on his torso and piercing his armor.

The Nephilim cries in rage, twisting and throwing the Amarok through the air. The monster crashes into the wall, knocking out load-bearing timbers and scattering the contents of the fireplace across the room. Marv stands across the blaze from the rest of us.

Suraz, on one knee, jams his blade into the ground to keep his feet. White blood pumps from the holes left by the Amarok's teeth.

The creature howls. I hear its claws scrabbling in the dirt before it smashes aside more timbers and charges back at Suraz. They collide and fly through the wall, out of the cabin.

Forget animal control. Marv needs an entire construction crew for this place now.

"Out!" I yell, as a beam crashes to the ground not a foot away from me.

"The Wendigo!" Diana screams, voice shrill. "They're still out there!"

"Marv holds 'em in thrall. They'll die when he does. Until he returns, anyway. Gives us time to skiddaddle."

Maybe Marv's death will give us the chance we need to reach the Mustang. He's doomed now, trapped by the flames, the cabin collapsing around him. If I can make it back to Haven, I might be able to gather more weapons and wait for his ghost. Then I can Expunge his ass.

Unbidden laughter bubbles from my throat. Through the flames, a shadow emerges, the fire caressing his skin but leaving him unharmed.

It's him.

I remember Charon's words in the woods. *Death lays at the end of your path, Fateless.*

The Ferryman may not see my end, but someone's death has called him here. I won't let it be Rosa's. I'll kill Marv myself, consequences be damned.

The cabin creaks, groans. Wood splinters, debris falls. Marv approaches, face ruined by the crucifix. His unholy tattoos pop from his flesh like a shield. I see the opening and charge.

The stone fireplace topples. I slam into Marv, hit him low and drive him back. My shoulder hits his solar plexus and blows the air out of him. His back hits the hearth and I spin away, a last roll of the dice to avoid a crushing death.

A rafter drops in front of me, just where I stood not one second before. Ol' Marv ain't so lucky.

The fireplace crumples as the walls and roof give in. They collapse, burying the bastard in a heap of stone and wood. I see him pulverized by block after block, bursting like a wet sack, bones shattering. Then he's buried. Gone.

The dust settles, but the fire's spreading. The cabin continues to groan and burn, and I hope to God that Rosa and the kid got clear. But I'm trapped.

At first, I think it's my imagination. I half-expect Marv to burst from the rubble, but no one could survive that. Right?

The flames surrounding me slow, so much I can see them flicker one way, then the other. They make no noise now. In fact, it's like sound's ceased to exist. The cabin's not hot or cold, and it should be one or the other with the flames running rampant and the gaping holes everywhere.

From the heap, a vapor rises. Grey, washed-out. It swirls in the air, draws together. From the formless shape, Marvin Clancy Junior reassembles.

I bare my teeth, tell my muscles to move, to grab his spirit before it can do anything, but they don't listen. I shouldn't be here. I'm inside a pocket, a reality outside of time, outside of the rules of Hell, a place between life and death. And it's because of him.

Charon.

The darkness that perverts the light around him floods through me, surrounds me, protects me—I'm certain he didn't mean it; he doesn't even seem to realize I'm here—and he steps forward, through me. My skin, my bones, my blood—they flush hot, then cold as winter, as he passes through my body, striding towards Marv's ghost. Awareness already flickers in the bastard's eyes.

"Welcome to eternity," Charon whispers, though I hear his voice reverberate in my head, like I'm thinking the words he speaks. "We met before, many years ago, though most forget my words. I told you then we would meet again, one final time, and your death would hold great meaning. You did not fail me. In fact, you surpassed my wildest expectations with your depravity."

"Lucifer?" Marv gasps, dropping to his knees.

"No," Charon replies. The darkness that trails him swells, like a wave held back by a dam, and it seeps into me, stops the flames from devouring me, holds the cabin from turning my body to paste. "I am much more than that. Come. The Seal awaits you."

Dark tendrils rush forward, then spread out, swallowing the flames and Marv's mist. They fill my sight.

A laugh like crunching gravel. *The Seal awaits you all…* Charon's voice blooms in my mind. *Next time, your friend will not be here to save your soul. Be seeing you.*

Then, silence.

Blinking, my vision returns. Marv's gone. So's Charon. The cabin's a burnt-out ruin. I turn, bones creaking like I haven't used them in eons.

The Ferryman's words echo in my mind, the ones from

Meadow Park, what seems like an age ago. *You think Hell is how you perceive it? Do you believe the dead linger here for no purpose, and only where you observe them? Foolish human.*

What a way to back up your words, Charon. It's clear I understand jack-shit.

"My friend?"

My hand's cold. Like ice. Diana's holding it, peering up at me with her hollow eyes.

"I heard him, Nick. But don't worry, I'll always be here to save you."

Behind me, Suraz stands with Rosa, their stares fixed on me. Wonder of wonders, the Nephilim looks away when I meet his eyes. Reckon he saw Charon too. I notice more puncture marks in his armor. He's taken a real beating, but Marv's gone. The Wendigo are gone. That Amarok's fucking dead at last.

Rosa smiles, tears spilling down her cheeks. I gasp, exhausted, and shiver. I almost fall to the floor. The kid takes my other hand and pulls me back up.

I meet that eyeless stare, ignore the crusted blood covering her face, and picture the child she used to be.

"How? I should have died in that fire."

Diana looks over her shoulder at Suraz. He still won't meet my eyes. He's gazing at the spot where Charon disappeared, but I can't tell if that's what he's thinking about. I shouldn't even try to imagine a Nephilim's thoughts.

"He told me to grab you, to tell the flames to die, where the debris should fall. I...didn't know if I could do it, but... I never wanted anything more."

"You're special, kid. You know that?"

A smile.

"Let's go home, Nick."

"No, kid. Gotta job to do, remember? Gotta lead and I promised you we'd see it through."

I squeeze her fingers.

"Time for you to get some closure."

THE END

We drive back to Haven as the night turns to dawn. Rosa sleeps with her head on my shoulder. Feels good. Feels right. Wanted to take her to hospital, or home at least, but she insisted that she come with. I agreed, as long as she waited in the car.

Parking the Mustang, I shift Rosa aside, gentle-like, so she doesn't wake up. Diana follows. We're at the Church of St. Francis on Haven's south side.

"You ready, kid?"

She nods and moves forward. Diana hasn't said a word since I told her about Zia's message and the information she gave me.

The church is basic, small. Daffodils grow in the gardens outside, and I ignore the ghosts drifting around. Holy ground's a nexus to Hell's spirits, even the Aware ones. They linger, as if they can find a way into Heaven if they stay there long enough.

Diana walks slow, and I'm grateful. Marv battered me. I'm limping and exhausted, but that's the least of my worries. In the car, while Diana looked inward and Rosa slept, I thought about Marv, how the Ferryman took his ghost, the words he said, and how I felt like a part of that moment.

Suraz didn't stick around. He took off before I could corner him and start with the questions.

The Seal. What in Hell is the Seal? And Charon saying Marv 'surpassed his wildest expectations'? I thought I learned the truth about Hell five years ago. Turns out I'd only scratched the surface. There's so much more to learn, and I better do it quick. Something's coming.

But first things first...

We enter the church. The aisle leads to a simple altar, pews on either side, and stations of the cross line the walls. Morning light streams through painted glass, and god rays fall on a priest with his head bowed at the foot of the dais.

"Let me do the talking," I whisper to Diana.

Like she has a choice, unless the priest's like me, but what I really mean is none of that psychokinetic shit. Not until I say the word.

The kid stares at the priest's back—he ain't noticed us—before turning to me. She gives a tight shake of her head.

"He deserves death."

I grimace, glance around to make sure no one sees me chatting with my invisible friend, then place both hands on Diana's shoulders, ignoring the chill.

"No doubt. Kid, it's your call, but you know what? Don't damn your soul. This is vengeance. Take it from me, that's an eternity's sentence."

"You said it yourself, Nick. Charon told you I'm in Hell forever."

"Bullshit." I shake my head, trying to make sense of the

last few days. "You stole to feed your family. Anyone would do the same. He expects me to believe human courts understand extenuating circumstances, but the Almighty doesn't? There's sinning and then there's folks like Marv..." I point to the priest. "...folks like him. They ain't the same, and I swear to you, we'll find a way to make things right, return you to your family. The two of us, remember? We'll figure things out."

Diana swings her head towards the priest. "Let's just do this."

I sigh, and straighten my back, which is harder than it sounds with the state I'm in. "Sure."

We approach the priest, dressed in his white cassock. I can already see he's a bigger guy, about the same size as me. Stocky, thick. Must run in the family.

"Father Clancy?" I call, coming to stand a few paces away. He looks over his shoulder, and I can see why Diana found Marv familiar. Resemblance is uncanny. "Father *Marvin* Clancy?"

Zia's text gave me the name and date of birth, October 1st 1947. I knew this wasn't our Marv, the Devil Worshipper. Too old. But, like I said, I quit believing in coincidences.

Diana's killer, the one who sparked a riot that claimed the kid's family and countless others? The man who lived in my apartment, got married and had a child before becoming a priest? Marvin Clancy Junior's father.

Small fucking world.

"Yes, my child? Have you come for confession?" He pushes himself up. Despite his size, he's frail. Father Clancy's face is kind. He smiles at me until he realizes my condition—

battered, dirty, crusted with blood—and the congeniality slips. "Are you in trouble, child?"

Beside me, Diana jerks forward. I throw out an arm, holding it against her chest. My forearm flashes with ice.

"Not anymore," I smile. "Name's Nick Holleran, P.I. Got asked to work a cold case. Real old. Ran into a couple of people you know."

Clancy shakes his head, goes to walk away. "I think you must have me mistaken with someone else, Mr. Holleran."

"Marvin Clancy Junior. Know him? Know how he got his kicks?"

The color doesn't drain from the priest's face; it disappears in an instant. Somehow, he looks even older. He sags, staggers a little. A part of me wants to steady him, but I know Diana would never forgive me. Gotta remember the things this old man did, the acts he tried to hide by joining the church, how he thought that absolved him.

"What has he done?" Father Clancy asks, voice flat.

"Just what all the kids are doing these days. Kidnapped a lady, tried to summon the Devil, murdered a whole bunch of people and enslaved their souls. That kind of thing."

The priest crosses himself. "The police have him?"

I hesitate, glance at Diana. Her jaw's tight, fists bunched at her sides.

"He's dead."

His legs crumple beneath him as he collapses on the stairs, hand on his chest. "Dear God, he's paid for my sins. Why not me? Why not *me*? My boy never stood a chance."

"Enough," Diana snarls. Her hands shoot out in front of her, pushing Father Clancy up the stairs with the force of her will. He screams, eyes wild, as the unseen force sends him crashing into the altar and pins him there.

"Diana," I warn, walking beside her as she bears down on the old man, "there's gotta be another way."

She scowls. Father Clancy sags a little. Kid's still got hold of him, but she's not going to tear him apart or crush him like a soda can under heel. I crouch down in front of Marvin Senior and meet his eyes.

The name haunts his lips. "Diana?"

"You blame yourself for your son's evil?" I ask. He has the same black stare as his son. Instead of malice, his is filled with regret.

"Who are you?" Clancy asks, mouth slack. "How are you doing this?"

"I'm sure your son told you he could see things."

"Madness. My boy was sickened. That's all."

"How did he die? As a child, I mean. Was that when it started?"

Father Clancy doesn't answer. Beside me, Diana squeezes her fist. The priest gasps for air, eyes bulging. I hold up my finger, and the kid stops. She's like Darth fucking Vader. Guess that makes me the Emperor?

"It started long before," he croaks. "Even God makes mistakes. I'd already turned to Him for absolution. I prayed for my boy's soul, but he was corrupt. Vile. My wickedness infected him. I should never have brought life into the world. But when he killed his mother," he wheezes, his words coming in a frenzy, "I pushed him down the stairs. I still recall that sound, the crunch of bone. I thought his neck had broken. I...thought I'd done it. Killed him. Saved us all. But, when he returned to life, raving about ghosts and creatures, I knew the Devil had taken him. Faith was the only way to fight, so I took up the cloth. I devoted my life to Him. To absolution."

I glance around the silent church, then up at the painted glass above me. This is a place of saints and angels, but the only folk here are three sinners.

"He lies," Diana growls. "He wanted to smother his son the day he was born, and so many times after. He enjoyed what he did to me and the others. He thinks about it when he pretends to pray."

Hot anger floods my chest. I tamp it down. Don't wanna egg the kid on. She's out for blood.

"What's it you priests like to say? 'Confession is the path to forgiveness'? You ever try that?"

"It's t-too late," Father Clancy stammers, tears running down his lined face.

"The case I'm working. About a girl who lived at Redwood and Maine..."

The priest grows still, silent. His tears slow to a trickle. Clancy licks his lips, eyes furtive. "Diana..."

"Yes."

"How? They're all..."

The priest trails off, and a shadow crosses his expression. He reminds me so very much of his son. The kind look in those black eyes is gone, and a trace of the old predator surfaces.

This sack of shit didn't change, didn't turn to God. He hid in a place he thought no one would come looking. Almost got away with it too.

"Remember the things your son told you?" I say, raising a finger. "It's all true."

I point at Clancy, and Diana forces her will on him, pushing him tighter against the altar. He screams through gritted teeth, the thin flesh on his face rippling like he's sat on the front seat of a rollercoaster. I touch Diana on the shoulder. She snarls, but relents.

"It's all a show," the kid hisses. "I feel him, Nick. That evil… He's a monster. Worse than his son. The Devil didn't make him that way; his father did!"

I know better than to doubt Diana's intuition, so I decide to press harder.

"The girl you killed, Diana Charles. The one you kidnapped, held in your room, tortured, tore her eyes out when she looked at you because of the shame. The one whose entire family died, along with the rest of the souls living at Redwood and Maine, because her momma knew you took her. She's with me, right now. You think about her a lot, don't you? Don't think I didn't see that look in your eyes when you spoke her name. You remember her just fine."

"I remember them all!" Clancy screams, eyes bulging. He laughs, a hysterical howl. "The Devil, he made me do it. Whispered to me, all the while, telling me what to do. I tried to change! I did! I swear to you."

I sock him in the nose. Hard. I grab the front of his cassock and haul him up. "Confess, you sick son of a bitch."

He giggles, red spittle dribbling down his chin. "Women. Always women, but I liked children most. How they'd scream, how'd they'd shake when I stood over them. Especially the ni—"

I hit him again, splitting my knuckles on his teeth, looming over him like he did to those kids. His mouth overflows. He laughs again.

"I took their eyes when they looked at me. The Devil told me to. He wanted—"

Another punch cuts him off. I pull him close, fist scrunched up in his robe, and stare into those black, feverish eyes. Wish I could kill this bastard myself. But that's not why I'm here. It's Diana's call, and if she decides to put this rabid dog down, I won't blame her.

"Trash like you are the reason the Devil walks in blood. But he doesn't ask for it and he sure as shit doesn't whisper it in your ear. I'm through with you."

I climb to my feet, turn my back on him, ignore the mad giggles mixing with his whimpers. Confession didn't absolve him; it broke him, and not before time. I meet Diana's empty stare.

"Do what you want, kid. Just remember what I said. You ain't like him. Or me."

I take a step away, close my eyes. I block out the screams from the priest as he yells for my attention. Maybe the kid's right and death's the only justice we can offer some people. After what he took from Diana, what he did to his victims, how he let that entire building of black families burn, how could anyone blame her for wanting revenge? I couldn't.

The thrill I felt when I Expunged the Wheelers, certain in my heart that I did the correct thing, tells me that.

"Nick?" The kid's voice penetrates my thoughts. Her hand's in mine, icy fingers tight. "We share the same pain. I've felt it since the moment I woke up in your office. Revenge isn't the way. Moving forward is. Call the cops, get him to confess. So long as he can't hurt another person, I don't care. I'm done here."

I turn. Father Clancy's still propped against the altar, breath coming in ragged gulps. She stopped herself. I lay a hand on her head, stroke her hair. The kid smiles.

Pulling out my cell, I approach the priest.

"You're in luck. You get to pay for your crimes after all. Tell the cops everything, before we change our minds."

Father Clancy nods, tears mingling with the blood on his cheeks, and it occurs to me I know a couple of cops who'd be very interested in this confession. Maybe they'll even do me a favor and get off my back.

I dial.

"Lori, it's Nick Holleran. You got Henry with you? Perfect, put me on speaker. There's a reason I ain't been around much. Got hired to work a cold case and I reckon I cracked it. You're gonna wanna talk to this guy." I press the cell to Father Clancy's ear. "Go ahead. Confession's good for the soul."

GETTING BETTER

Marvin Senior's going to spend the twilight of his life in prison. He confessed to the murder of fourteen girls and women, six of them black, dating between 1965 and 1970. He led the cops to where he'd buried the bodies, didn't even try to defend himself in court. Wonder what Charon's going to say to him when he finally passes.

Taking stock of the last few days makes my head spin. I survived Wendigo, a possessed Amarok, and a Devil Worshipper. I met Lucifer himself and rekindled an old flame. I'm in Hell, surrounded by ghosts, demons, cults and creatures from every myth and legend I ever heard, but I'm getting by, with a little help from my friends.

Lori and Henry have given me space, only calling into my office to give me the faintest of shakedowns and the most grudging thank you I ever heard. My wounds healed well, and each time I've spied Suraz watching me, he's nodded.

No Charon, either, though I reckon it ain't the last I've seen of him.

Jim, the skin-walker, stopped by after my run-in with the Wendigo, and he gave me a well-earned fee that'll go some way towards making my life a little cozier. Even bought a gift for Diana. Call it a housewarming present.

Kid's living with me now. She's not too hot on visiting my office again yet, but I've grown used to having her around, and where else would she go? For her part, she's delved into studying anything she can about Hell, pestering Ruby whenever she sees her, asking me to get books from Harry and Maeve's. It's great to see her motivated. Can already tell she's going to be amazing at this.

And Rosa?

My apartment door swings open, and there she stands. She ain't living with me, but she stayed over last night. Couple of days after the cabin, once she'd recovered, we talked. One of those conversations about everything and nothing that goes on long into the night and only ends when the sun rises.

She's stayed over twice since.

"You get it?" she asks, face breaking into a grin.

I heft the package under my arm. "Got it."

"She's gonna love it," Rosa says, kissing me on the cheek. "Mail came while you were out."

It's funny. Rosa can't see Diana, hasn't spoken to her without me or Ruby as a go-between, but she cares for the kid. Don't know how she manages to make a surreal situation seem so natural. It lights Diana up, feeling how genuine Rosa is towards her.

I notice the mound of mail on my breakfast counter. Bills, no doubt. They can wait.

"Hey kid, get out here. Wanna show you something."

I set the package down next to the mail, and a handwritten address catches my eye. Diana comes out of the bedroom—says she enjoys time alone sometimes; typical teenager, huh?—and smiles when she sees me. Her grin goes wider when she sees the box.

"Is that for me? What is it?"

I wink, open the box, and pull out the record player, just like the one Diana's family used to have—an authentic 1960s Champion.

"Hope you like it, kid."

Diana gapes. "Nick, it's... It's *perfect*."

"Figured you needed some furniture of your own, since you're staying. Wanna set it up by the window?" She floats the player across the room and I smirk as I reach into my jacket. "That's not all, figured you wouldn't have heard this."

I pull out a vinyl copy of *The White Album* by The Beatles and present it to her.

"Came out after you moved on. Thought you might like to catch up. Hey, if I'd known you were a Beatles fan, maybe I wouldn't have kept you listening to Nirvana so long."

"I guess they weren't so bad," she said, breaking into a grin, "but they *were* imitators."

I think back six days, to when Diana fixed to kill a man. I've no doubt Marvin Senior deserves death, but the kid wasn't the one to dish it out. She's innocent, even if God don't agree. One day, I'll prove it to him.

"I love this album," Rosa says, taking it from me. "I'll set it up, big guy. Looks like you've plenty of admin to do."

I grin, and grab the mail. The handwritten one comes first. Don't recognize the writing. I tear it open, reading through as *Back In The U.S.S.R.* scratches into life. Shock slaps me, and a bizarre feeling starts to unfold in my stomach. I shake my head and read again. Must be a mistake.

"Nick?" Rosa calls, concern on her face. "What is it?"

I hand her the letter. "It's from a lawyer's firm. Harry and Maeve, they left it all to me. Their research, their library, their home. Everything."

Rosa crashes into me, hugging me tight. I hug her back and laugh as Diana dances to The Beatles. Two weeks ago, I thought I had life and death figured out. No one knew it better. Now, I realize my journey through Hell's just beginning, and even though I've got one life left, thanks to my friends, I got a real chance of making something of it. I kiss Rosa before she pulls away to dance. I hold the letter in my heart, and I ain't ashamed to say tears well in my eyes.

I need a minute. Just to let this sink in. Picking up my carton of smokes, I leave the girls to The Beatles and take my leave. They'll understand.

In silence, I head down the stairs and outside, back into Hell. There's still that weight in the air, that sickness on the wind, the distracted, glum, and apathetic faces passing by, but right now, the skies are blue, as far as the eye can see.

"I'll see you again," I say to Harry and Maeve, and the only cloud I see is a grey one on the horizon, "and we'll have one Hell of a party."

"Perhaps that is where your fate leads you, Nick Holleran, but I think not."

And I hadn't even lit my cigarette yet.

Charon's standing beside me, his cloak of shadow surrounding him. I study the cloud again. A sign of ill omen in the future maybe, but it's better than staring into those almost-human eyes.

"Thought I'd have seen you sooner after the business at the cabin. Heard what you said to Marv. Still remember it too."

Silence. I glance at the Ferryman. He's cocked his head, puzzlement plain on that craggy face.

"That is not possible," he grates, his voice like a coffin dragged across stone.

"What's the Seal, Charon? Why are you taking ghosts there?"

It starts as a wheeze. His shoulders shake beneath his black coat, and the shadows surrounding him writhe as he laughs.

"One day, Fateless, when your time comes to end, I will take you there, and you'll find out for yourself. Our business is *not* at an end. Be seeing you, Nick Holleran."

He steps back into the shadows and they welcome him like a lover. On the horizon, more grey clouds have gathered, and they're moving in fast.

"You bet your ass, you sonofabitch," I mutter, cigarette between my lips. A sudden wind picks up, makes my lighter's flame flicker as I light up. "And I'm not going out without a fight. I'll make my own goddamned fate."

As I drag on the cigarette, Hell stirs. I've got a lot to learn, but Lord knows I'll learn it fast. There's a Seal out there—something big, something important. I'll find it, and I'll figure the Ferryman out, if it's the last thing I do.

Rain falls, and the temperature plummets. I stamp out my smoke beneath my heel and head back inside.

Be seeing you, Charon.

EPILOGUE

A BEGINNING

The city moves around me. The humans are oblivious to a Nephilim and the Devil standing in their midst as we look up at Nick Holleran's apartment. I haven't stopped watching him since that night in the cabin, though he knows to look for me. The Fateless, as Charon calls him.

"You're recovering?" Lucifer asks. He leans against the wall of a building and wears a faint smile as the living pass him by. He seems almost fond of them.

"Hm," I grunt. My battles with the Wendigo wearied me, and the wounds the Amarok gave me still ache, though I've suffered worse.

"Fine," Lucifer sighs. "Ask your questions."

"The girl," I say, thinking of Holleran's eyeless companion. "She picked her time in becoming Aware, did she not?"

The Devil grins. "I may have given her a nudge."

"Why?"

Lucifer pushes himself off the wall and moves beside me. How small I feel in his presence, how unworthy, how he reminds me of the things I have lost and how I long for so much more.

"Charon. What does he say of Holleran?"

"He calls him the Fateless."

Lucifer snaps his fingers. "Yes. Suraz, we are governed by laws, fate and destiny, since before we existed. The rebellion against my brother had been preordained, and so is Armageddon. You might call me an actor, carrying out my role. Charon claims to see all this. All that has been, all that is and all that will be. Time is different for him, but Holleran? He sees nothing. Doesn't that interest you?"

There's a fire behind Lucifer's golden eyes, which I have not seen since we stood before the gates of Mezzala, God's palace in Heaven.

"You have not answered my question."

Lucifer bares his teeth. "No. I want to push him, Suraz. See what happens when one without a Fate blazes his way through Hell. The Seal swells, my friend. I can't keep it whole forever. The more Charon feeds it, the stronger it becomes. Once the Seal breaks, the layers of Hell will break open. A showdown with my brother approaches. I will lead them into Heaven again, but not before the time is right. We're not ready for war. My instincts tell me Holleran is key. He's nothing like his parents, and for that, I'm grateful."

"You knew them?"

Lucifer pauses, a tiny crease between his eyebrows forming. "Oh, yes. Those people I held no fondness for."

"Your love of the humans led you here in the first place, Lucifer."

"And your love of me made you follow, Suraz."

He places a hand against my face. My skin sings at his touch. I haven't felt it in too long. It transports me back to a time when we were more than servant and master, more than friends. For a moment, I almost relent, but how can I walk such a path again?

Lucifer turns, striding away, taking my longing with him. I watch until he's out of sight, before turning on my heel and walking in the opposite direction. My destination nears, the Church of St Michael's. Such a fight we had, Michael and I. The only warrior to defeat me in combat. Now, with my body craving alcohol and narcotics, I wager he wouldn't break a sweat in smiting me.

I enter the cathedral, its vaulted ceiling domed, its aisle wide. I kneel at the altar, head bowed, but I turn my eyes upward, and watch as the God rays streaming through the glass glow brighter, until a figure steps out of them.

Metatron. The highest of angels, and God's favored.

I avert my eyes as he approaches—better that than to earn his displeasure, his anger. The angel's white armored boots stop before me.

"Look at me," he whispers. A soft voice, but I find it impossible to disobey.

My eyes settle on his lips. Even with his invitation, I won't meet his eyes. I am not worthy. He has made that clear in the past. Metatron gazes at me, his obsidian skin darker from the pure white of his armor and hair. Though he smiles, I see his golden eyes holding scorn at the edges of my vision.

"What news?"

"Lucifer has grown obsessed with one named Nick Holleran, the Fateless. He says he's key in his war with our God."

Metatron taps at his lip with a finger, deep in thought.

"He plans to attack then. When?"

I hesitate. "He did not share that with me. He grows concerned that the Seal will break soon, that Armageddon approaches. He says he is not ready. Does this please you?"

I cringe at the pathetic words I say, the plain need to please in my voice. Metatron smiles.

"You have done well, Suraz. Watch this Fateless, and if he appears a danger to God's realm, remove him from the board. Return when you have more news."

"Wait," I say, stretching out my arm. Metatron pauses, but he doesn't look back. "You will speak to God for me, tell him of the work I do?"

"My old friend," Metatron says, moving into the light. "Rest assured, God hears all you say."

The angel returns to Heaven. I watch God's light return to the normal light of Hell, and tears flow down my face, dripping onto my armor.

Lucifer has been more than a friend to me for eons. But I know, deep in my heart, that the Devil will never take Heaven, and I cannot remain in Hell much longer, though my betrayal rips me apart and eats at my soul with a hunger no drug can take away. I climb to my feet, resigned to my task. To learn of Lucifer's plans, to watch the Fateless.

Nick Holleran has one life left, and if it means my return to God's grace, I will not hesitate in taking it.

'Behold, I stand at the door and knock. If anyone hears my voice and opens the door, I will come in to him and eat with him, and he with me.'
— Revelations, 3:20.

THE END

Nick Holleran will return in *One Life Left* in 2022

David Green is a writer of dark fiction. Born in Manchester, UK and living in Galway, Ireland, David grew up with gloomy clouds above his head, and rain water at his feet, which has no doubt influenced his dark scribblings. David is the author of the Pushcart Prize nominated novelette Dead Man Walking, and is excited for his fantasy series, Empire of Ruin, debuting in June 2021 from Eerie River Publishing.

Newsletter: https://tinyurl.com/y6ah8brp
www.twitter.com/davidgreenwrite
www.davidgreenwriter.com
https://www.facebook.com/davidgreenwriter

AFTERWORD

The dark cloud on the horizon swirls and thickens, stretching out across the sky as Hell stirs below it. Nick knows something approaches... and so do the other major players.

Lucifer's passion is reignited, but does he know about his most loyal friend's betrayal? What lay in the makeshift graves dug by Nick's parents, so long ago, and why does the Devil know them? And just what is Charon's game? The Seal weakens, the forces of Heaven and Hell move on a collision course, and standing in between them is Nick Holleran, a man who thought he had death figured out.

He doesn't and he needs to learn fast.

I hope you found The Devil Walks In Blood enjoyable; the dynamic of Nick and Diana was one that excited me from when I wrote about the 'ghost in the corner' when sketching out Dead Man Walking, and delving into it was a pure pleasure for me. Bringing Rosa into the mix was always part of the plan; she's a character that grounds Nick and his story, and one who will have plenty to come in further installments.

At the moment, there's three more stories planned. Yes, the Nick Holleran series has an end point, a goal in mind, with fates for the characters set in stone. Even 'The Fateless.' Unlike Dead Man Walking, there's no tip-off point for the next case, but there are hints at what is to come next... why not go read it again and we can discuss your theories? Nothing would make me happier.

Thank you for reading, and if you would, please take the time to review on Amazon, Goodreads and anywhere else that will take your words. Reviews are the life-blood of an author, and word of mouth helps get Nick out there.

Holleran will return. Soon. *With one life left*, he needs to tread with care.

Until next time,
David Green.

ACKNOWLEDGMENTS

First of all, my erstwhile beta-reader and first port-of-call who checks that what I've written makes basic sense: Chris Hewitt. The pages came in thick and fast for this one!

Michelle at Eerie River Publishing for giving Nick a new home and pushing me to hone the story further; thank you.

S.O. Green, my fabulous editor, for smoothing off the edges and for laser-focused insight.

All of you who read the original Dead Man Walking; your excitement and enthusiasm made writing this one easier.

And to my son, Ollie, the reason I do all of this. There's a scene just for you in book three. I promise!

More from Eerie River

Eerie River Publishing, is a small independant publishing house that is devoted to releasing quality dark fiction books and anthologies.

To stay up to date with all our new releases and upcoming giveaways, follow us on Facebook, Twitter, Instagram and YouTube. Sign up for our monthly newsletter and receive a free ebook Darkness Reclaimed, as our thank you gift.

https://mailchi.mp/71e45b6d5880/welcomebook

Interested in becoming a Patreon member?
Patreon membership gives you exclusive sneak peeks at upcoming books, early chapter releases, covers art as well as free ebooks and discounts on paperbacks.

https://www.patreon.com/EerieRiverPub.

ALSO AVAILABLE FROM
EERIE RIVER PUBLISHING

NOVELS/NOVELLAS
Storming Area 51: Horror At the Gate
SENTINEL
In Solitudes Shadow

ANTHOLOGIES/SERIES
AFTER: A Post-Apocalyptic Survivor Series
It Calls From The Forest: Volume I
It Calls From The Forest: Volume II
It Calls From The Sky
Darkness Reclaimed
With Blood and Ash
With Bone and Iron

DRABBLE COLLECTIONS
Forgotten Ones: Drabbles of Myth and Legend
Dark Magic: Drabbles of Magic and Lore

COMING SOON
The Void
A Sword Named Sorrow
It Calls From the Doors

www.EerieRiverPublishing.com

Also by David Green
In Solitude's Shadow

This hard-hitting dark fantasy series is already gaining fantastic reviews from authors like A.M. Justice, Lou Yardly and Jason Nugent. Not only that but reviewers like Blaise from FanFiAddict said " This is without a doubt the best fantasy novella I have read since The Emperor's Soul by Brandon Sanderson."

Available in paperback, hardcover and ebook.

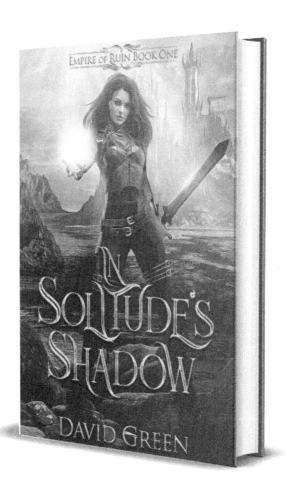

Printed in Great Britain
by Amazon

THE DEVIL WALKS IN BLOOD
BY DAVID GREEN